CLAUDIA'S ~~FREIND~~ FRIEND

I sighed. I should have known my best friend would sense that things weren't going too well for me. "Mrs Hall told me that if I don't get a good grade, a really good grade, in the English test coming up two weeks from Wednesday, I'm going to fail English."

"Oh, no!" gasped Mary Anne.

"You need to get some help," said Kristy briskly.

"No kidding," I said, depression washing over me. "Especially since a big part of the test is going to be spelling and vocabulary."

"How about the resource room?" said Dawn neutrally.

"No! I mean, I don't have to go, yet. But if I don't pass this test . . ."

"Wait a minute!" Stacey leaned forward. "What about us?"

"I don't know," I said. "What about you?"

"Tutoring you! We're tutoring Shea. Why couldn't we tutor you?"

CLAUDIA'S ~~FREIND~~ FRIEND

Ann M. Martin

Hippo

Scholastic Children's Books,
7-9 Pratt Street, London NW1 0AE, UK
a division of Scholastic Publications Ltd,
London ~ New York ~ Toronto ~ Sydney ~ Auckland

First published in the US by Scholastic Inc., 1993
First published in the UK by Scholastic Publications Ltd, 1995

ISBN 0 590 55951 6

Typeset in Plantin by Contour Typesetters, Southall, London
Printed by Cox & Wyman Ltd, Reading, Berks

10 9 8 7 6 5 4 3 2 1

*The author gratefully acknowledges
Nola Thacker
for her help in preparing this manuscript.*

1st CHAPTER

I was trying to look on the bright side. It was Monday, true. But it was Monday *after-noon*. School was almost over for the day. Just a couple more classes and I was home and free. Well, not free. I had a babysitting job after school and my friends and I would go to our usual Babysitters Club meeting at 5.30. But I like babysitting and BSC meetings. After all, I'm a good babysitter, and *I* am the vice-chairman of the BSC. But more about our club later. Anyway, at that moment I was posed in what I hoped was an I-am-an-interested-student way near the back of Mrs Hall's English class.

You might guess from the above comments that I'm not a model member of the student body at Stoneybrook Middle School, where I'm in the eighth grade. But I wouldn't say my pose was *all* a pose. I'm an interested student—when it comes to some things.

Like art. I love art. I take classes at school and extra art lessons after school. Some day I hope to be a great artist.

And junk food. I'm definitely an interested student of junk food. I even managed to combine these two interests—art and junk food—when I had my first private art show. It was held in my garage and it was called "Disposable Comestibles". That means I painted and drew quite a few pictures of Twixes, potato crisps and other foods with cool textures (and tastes). And to prove what a dedicated artist I am, I didn't eat a single subject until *after* I'd finished painting its portrait.

What else? Oh, yes. I suppose you could say I'm a student of fashion, too. I like clothes: colours, textures, surprises. (Which makes me a sort of ongoing work of art, I suppose.) But I do think I have a unique style, and a good one, too. In fact (although this may sound conceited), except for one other person at SMS, I think I'm the fashion queen, or princess, or whatever. The other person is Stacey, who's my best friend and the treasurer of the Babysitters Club.

Who am I? Well . . .

"Claudia? Claudia Kishi!" I jumped

about a mile. It was the mile from wherever my thoughts were to where my body was sitting in Mrs Hall's class.

"Huh?" I said.

I heard someone behind me snigger.

I braced myself for the rebuke I was sure Mrs Hall was going to hand out, but instead she just gave me a reproachful look and turned to survey the room. Several hands shot up, and I leaned back in my seat, embarrassed but relieved.

After that I tried to concentrate. I really did. But someone started reading a poem, and when I heard the title, which was "When I Am Old I Shall Wear Purple", my mind skipped to my grandmother Mimi.

Mimi was the person I was closest to in my family. I mean, I love my family. But my sister Janine is a genuine genius (she takes courses at the local college even though she's still in high school!) which makes her a little hard to communicate with sometimes. My parents, who are terrific, just don't understand why I'm not a good student. They're always saying things like, "Just put your mind to it, Claudia. If you'd concentrate on your studies just one tenth as much as you do on your art, you'd be a straight-A student."

But Mimi understood. She never tried to change me. She supported me and loved me just the way I was. And she *listened*. I'd go to her with problems and she'd let me talk about them without interrupting or telling me what I'd done wrong, or what I should do to make things right. Then she would look at me and say, "My Claudia, what to do?"

But Mimi's gone now. She had a stroke, and was ill for a while. Then, one day, she was gone.

I still miss her, my Mimi . . .

"Claudia?"

Oh, no. Mrs Hall was calling on me again!

But then I realized that the bell was ringing and everyone around me was standing up, and Mrs Hall was beckoning me towards her desk.

I quickly gathered up my books, stuffed them in my bag, and approached Mrs Hall's desk. I tried not to look as guilty as I felt about not hearing a word in class.

Mrs Hall studied me for a moment and I shifted nervously from one foot to the other.

Finally she said, "Claudia, as you know we have an English test coming up."

"I haven't forgotten," I said brightly. And I hadn't, really. I just hadn't been thinking about it. After all, it was only Monday.

And the test was a long way away. Plenty of time to worry later.

"Claudia, are you listening to me?" Mrs Hall was looking annoyed.

Hastily I replayed her last words in my head. "My performance," I repeated.

My performance. Uh-oh! This sounded ominous.

Mrs Hall nodded. "As it stands now, your performance in this class is not good. In fact, unless your spelling improves markedly, you are in danger of failing English this grading period."

"Failing!" I exclaimed. "Are you sure?"

It was a stupid question, of course, but my reaction seemed to make Mrs Hall a little more sympathetic. "I'm afraid so, Claudia. And half of this test will cover vocabulary and spelling. If you don't do well on this test—and I don't mean just pass, you'll have to do better than that— I'm sorry to say you will in all probability fail."

I couldn't think of much to say. Finally I settled for, "Oh."

Mrs Hall pressed her hands together and leaned towards me. "Claudia, why don't I arrange for you to spend some time in the resource room again? It's helped before."

I could think of what to say to *that*. "No!"

Mrs Hall looked a little startled, so I lowered my voice and tried to sound less panicked and more reasonable. "I mean, no, thank you. I don't think that will be necessary."

"What are you going to do, then?" asked Mrs Hall.

"I'll study," I promised. "I'll start tonight and I'll work hard. I really will."

Mrs Hall didn't look convinced, but she said, "Very well. However, if you do not pass this test, we will do more than just talk about using the resource room."

"Don't worry," I told Mrs Hall. "I'll be . . ." I searched my brain and actually came up with a vocabulary word. At least I think it was one. Or maybe it was just one of my sister Janine's usual words. "I'll be diligent, I promise."

I gave Mrs Hall a big, sincere smile and then hurried out before she could change her mind.

Don't worry, I'd told Mrs Hall. But it was something I couldn't tell myself.

I wasn't a very interested student for the rest of the afternoon, but this time, it wasn't because I was thinking about all the other interesting things I could be doing.

Oh, no. I was concentrating, concentrating on worrying about that test.

By the time the school day was over I was a wreck.

Fortunately it didn't show when I met the other members of the BSC on the steps outside school at the end of the last period. We all had sitting jobs that afternoon in my neighbourhood (business has been booming) and we'd decided to walk there together. Just seeing everybody made me feel better. We're all such different people that I don't need to compare myself to any of my friends. When I'm with my fellow BSC members—Kristy, Mary Anne, Dawn, Stacey, Jessi and Mallory—I can just be myself.

The point is we all have strengths and weaknesses and we know it, and we're all there for each other when we need to be. I suppose that's what friends are for, when you come to think of it.

Anyway, I felt better seeing my friends and knowing that they accept me for who I am and aren't going to think less of me for not being the world's best student.

I jumped down the last two front steps of the school and landed by Stacey.

She gave me a sideways glance and then said, "If I got a pair of purple Reeboks, could I do that?"

"Only if you have ankle socks with lavender lace trim." I grinned at her.

"It's a thought," said Stacey. "And a little step work might be just the thing for the Spring Dance."

"That's right!" I let go of my worries

about English. This was something much nicer to think about—the forthcoming Spring Dance at the Community Centre.

"Has anyone been invited yet?" Mallory wondered out loud. "Mary Anne, has Logan asked you?"

"Or have you asked Logan, Mary Anne?" put in Kristy.

"Does that mean *you're* asking Bart?" teased Mallory.

"Maybe," said Kristy loftily.

"I wonder if someone's brother is going to ask anyone," I said, looking around vaguely.

"I don't know if Sam knows about it," said Kristy bluntly, and next to me, I felt Stacey smile (if you know what I mean). Sam, who is Kristy's older brother, likes Stacey. He's teased her endlessly to prove it.

Mallory said, "I bet it'll be fun, no matter who we go with."

"Ben Hobart, Ben Hobart," whispered Jessi loudly.

Mallory blushed, but it didn't keep her from whispering back, "Curtis Shaller, Curtis Shaller."

"Well, I agree with you, Mallory," Mary Anne said. "We haven't done much at the Community Centre, but when we have been there it's been fun. And maybe I *will* ask Logan if he wants to go."

"Go for it," said Kristy.

"So do we dress up? Maybe borrow some of Karen's perfume?" I joked.

"Phew!" Dawn held her nose and we all laughed. During the summer holidays we had gone to Shadow Lake with Kristy's family. We went to a dance at the lodge there, and Karen (Kristy's little stepsister) and her two best friends, Nancy and Hannie, put on their best party clothes and about a gallon of "Lovely Lady" perfume. The perfume should have been called "Knock-Out", because that's what it almost did to us. And, even though the Three Musketeers (that's what Karen and Nancy and Hannie call themselves) changed into more casual clothes and washed some of the perfume off before the dance, they still had a very distinctive aura for the rest of the night.

I was giggling at the memory of the perfume disaster when Kristy said, "Dress up? What do you mean, dress up?" Kristy's a fully fledged tomboy, and a *dedicated* casual dresser. She almost always wears jeans, a polo-neck sweater and trainers.

I looked thoughtful. "Well, I was thinking of a long dress, high heels, maybe doing something really special with my hair."

Stacey caught on right away. "Excellent

idea, Claudia. I've got a terrific three-quarter length ballerina skirt and this cool crop top jacket."

"Skirts! Heels! I was thinking of maybe a special shirt to go with my good jeans." Kristy, our fearless BSC chairman, looked so alarmed that we couldn't help ourselves, and we started laughing. After a moment, she laughed, too.

"You got me," she admitted.

We laughed and talked all the way to our various jobs and by the time I was knocking on the door of my own babysitting job, I'd managed to put the English test worry to one side. I'd be seeing everybody again at our BSC meeting at 5.30. I could talk to them about it then. Between us, we'd come up with something, I was sure.

After all, if you can't count on your friends, who can you count on?

2nd
CHAPTER

Footsteps pounded up the stairs and a moment later Mallory burst into my room.

Kristy, who was sitting in a director's chair, her green visor on her head, looked pointedly at her watch. Our meetings are held on Mondays, Wednesdays and Fridays at my house from 5.30 to 6.00 p.m. and Kristy's a real stickler for punctuality. It goes with being hyper-organized, I suppose.

Anyway, it was 5.33. I smothered a grin, but Mallory didn't bother to try to hide her smile. "Sorry I'm late, but you *know* the job was until five-thirty, Kristy."

"True," said Kristy, relenting.

I handed Mallory the bag of sour cream and onion crisps I had pulled from behind my chest of drawers, and I opened a can of diet soda. A bag of trail-mix was also circling the room (Dawn and Stacey were busy raiding that), as well as a box of chocolate twigs. Those are little sticks of chocolate shaped like twigs, *not* real twigs dipped in chocolate!

"Subs!" said Stacey, and we all began the ritual groaning as we fished in our pockets and bags and purses. We pay subs every Monday, and that goes for club expenses. We pay Kristy's brother Charlie to drive her to and from the meetings, since she lives on the other side of town, and we pay for my phone bill, and occasionally we have a pizza party. We also use the money to buy supplies for our Kid-Kits. Kid-Kits are boxes we've decorated and filled with books and toys and games and stickers—pretty basic stuff, but a fun distraction, especially if you're going to a new client or it's a rainy day. Kids always like having new things to play with or to read. Kid-Kits are another one of Kristy's great ideas, just like the BSC . . .

No. I should begin at the beginning and tell you the story in coherent narrative form. I remembered that from English because it actually made sense. In art, the arrangement of your subjects (and colours and all kinds of other things) makes a statement. So it makes sense when you're telling a story to arrange what you say in some meaningful way.

Anyway, to begin at the beginning: my friends and I are in a club called the Babysitters Club. We started it because of one of Kristy Thomas's great ideas. One night she was listening to her mother trying to find a babysitter. Mrs Thomas made one phone call after another, but no one was available. That's when Kristy had this flash of brilliance. What if her mother could call one number and reach a whole lot of babysitters at once? Since Kristy and Mary Anne and Stacey and I were experienced babysitters, naturally we were perfect for the job.

So that's the beginning. Kristy became chairman of the Babysitters Club, I became vice-chairman, Mary Anne Spier became secretary, and Stacey McGill became treasurer. But soon we had more business than the four of us could handle. That's when Dawn Schafer joined us as alternate officer. And shortly after that, Mallory Pike and Jessica Ramsey joined us too, as junior officers, when Stacey moved to New York for a while. Oh, and I almost forgot Shannon Kilbourne and Logan Bruno. They're associate members. They don't come to meetings or pay subs, but they will take jobs when we can't.

So it's all clear now, right?

Well, almost. I just need to tell you who everyone is.

Kristy Thomas is, as you already know, super-organized, a low-profile dresser, and full of terrific ideas. This makes her the perfect chairman of the BSC. When she started the club, she still lived on Bradford Court, next door to Mary Anne, who was (and is) her best friend, and opposite me. But a little later, her mum got married to Watson Brewer, and Kristy and her older brothers Charlie and Sam and her younger brother David Michael moved into Watson's mansion. That's right—a real mansion, because Watson's a real millionaire!

Kristy wasn't thrilled at first, maybe because she missed her old neighbourhood and was used to her family of five. (Kristy's father left when she was little and she can hardly remember him.) But she could see the advantages, like having Watson, who's a pretty nice guy, for a stepfather. And she adores Watson's kids from his previous marriage, Karen and Andrew, who are seven and four. They live with their mother during the week and for some weekends, and with Watson for other weekends and some holidays.

Another advantage to living at Watson's is that there's plenty of room for everyone.

In fact there's so much room, the family adopted a new sister.

Emily Michelle is two and a half. She's Vietnamese, and Kristy's mum and Watson (Mr and Mrs Brewer, I suppose I should say, but it does feel weird, calling Mrs Brewer that when I've called her Mrs Thomas all my life, or most of it, anyway . . .) Now, where was I? Oh. So the Brewers adopted Emily Michelle. And then they asked Nannie, Kristy's maternal grand-mother, to come and stay with them and help out, and she did. There's also Boo-Boo, Watson's cross old cat, whose meow is as bad as his bite, and Shannon, a Bernese mountain dog puppy, who's as sweet as Boo-Boo is cranky.

I think it's a perfect set-up for Kristy. Plenty of scope for her organizational skills. If she sometimes seems bossy and very outspoken, well, in a big family you need a strong voice to be heard, right?

Now, having a strong voice isn't the way I'd describe Mary Anne Spier. But just because she's quiet and shy and small (she and Kristy are the shortest people in our eighth grade class) and very sensitive and tenderhearted, doesn't mean she isn't strong and strong-willed, too. For one thing, if she wasn't pretty strong-willed, I don't think she and Kristy could have stayed best friends. I mean, the fact that they are both short and have brown hair and brown eyes and were neighbours wouldn't be enough, because in so many ways they're opposites. For another thing, Mary Anne's mother died when she was a baby, and she was brought up by her father.

I've tried to imagine my family consisting of just me and my father, and I have to admit, it's pretty unimaginable. In fact, it would be pretty tough. But I suppose having only one parent would make you more independent.

Not that Mr Spier was a bad parent. He was just the opposite—extra-careful, extra-protective, extra-caring. So extra-everything that he treated Mary Anne like a baby for far too long. She was still wearing plaits and little-girl clothes when she was in seventh grade.

But finally Mary Anne had a talk with her father and he began to loosen up a little. He can still be strict, but he's changed. So has Mary Anne. She's wearing cooler clothes and a different hairstyle, and was allowed to get a kitten named Tigger. She even has a boyfriend, Logan Bruno.

To tell the truth, the whole Spier family has changed. Mr Spier got married—to Dawn Schafer's mother!

You see, Dawn's mother and father

divorced, and Mrs Schafer moved from California back to her old hometown of Stoneybrook with Dawn and Dawn's younger brother Jeff. Then Dawn and Mary Anne became friends. (Dawn became Mary Anne's other best friend, which was a problem for Kristy at first, but that has worked out because a person can have more than one best friend, right?) Anyway, Mary Anne persuaded Kristy that Dawn was a perfect candidate for the BSC. *Then* Mary Anne and Dawn were looking through these old yearbooks and discovered that Mr Spier and Mrs Schafer had been high school sweethearts! So they got their parents together and Mr Spier and Mrs Schafer fell in love all over again. This time they got married. Unfortunately, Jeff had become very homesick, and decided to move back to California to live with his dad. So now Mary Anne and Tigger and her father live with Dawn and her mother in this great old farmhouse that even has a haunted (maybe) secret passage!

Which is perfect for Dawn. Dawn has long, long pale blonde hair, two earrings in each ear, a genuine love of health food (yuck!), and an equally genuine dislike of junk food (eek!). Dawn is about as no-nonsense and straightforward and laid-back as you can get—but she loves ghost stories. I think she *really believes* in ghosts.

Still, maybe it is sort of laid-back to believe in ghosts, and at the same time live calmly in the same house as one!

Calm *and* tough are two words I'd use to describe Stacey McGill. She's my best friend, the first real best friend I've ever had, and I naturally think she's pretty terrific. Like Mary Anne, Stacey's an only child. And like Kristy and Dawn, her parents are divorced. Like Dawn and Jessi, she moved here from somewhere else (New York City). And like me, she appreciates the subtleties of fashion. And of course she's a maths whiz. She also has the most tremendous will power, because like Dawn, she doesn't eat junk food. But that isn't because Stacey doesn't like it. She'd love to dig into a bag of marshmallows, or polish off some Twixes. Only she can't.

Stacey is diabetic. That means her body doesn't handle sugar very well. She has to be very careful about what she eats, and give herself injections of insulin every day or she could get really, really ill.

When Mr and Mrs McGill found out Stacey had diabetes, they became as over-protective as Mary Anne's father. Stacey had to prove to her parents that she could handle her illness responsibly. And she did.

Things are less tense now. But she still has to be careful.

In terms of appearance, Stacey emanates this New York aura. She's blonde and blue-eyed, and very sophisticated looking, and probably a little more mature than the rest of us. She's totally into clothes, and *almost* as wild as I am about trying out different styles. Sometimes she'll get her hair permed just for an experiment. Her style is different, though. For example, she's allowed to wear make-up, and does, but in an understated way that really works. And while I'm dedicated to never wearing the exact same outfit twice (even if that only means wearing different earrings), Stacey has these great co-ordinated outfits that are wardrobe staples. But she doesn't wear the same clothes all the time. She likes to experiment with new looks, too.

Mallory Pike and Jessica Ramsey, who are in sixth grade at SMS and our junior officers, are also the youngest members of the BSC. In fact, Mallory used to be one of our babysittees. She's the oldest of eight children (even more kids than in Kristy's family), three of whom are triplets! We noticed while babysitting that Mallory was more like another babysitter than one of the kids, and when our business grew enough so that we needed more babysitters, we asked her. She and Jessi can only sit during weekend days and in the afternoons after school, but that's fine, because it frees us for other jobs.

Like Mary Anne and Stacey, Mallory has had to give her parents a little nudging to persuade them to treat her like the responsible person she is. She finally persuaded them to let her have her ears pierced (one hole in each ear) and she's working on getting contact lenses so she won't have to wear glasses.

Mallory was practically the first person Jessi met when she moved to Stoneybrook. They have some basic things in common: they're both the oldest kids in their families, they both love to read, particularly horse stories and especially the ones by Marguerite Henry, and they are both talented. But like Kristy and Mary Anne, they're pretty different, too.

How? Well, Mallory has lived in Stoneybrook all her life, but Jessi moved here from New Jersey. Mallory wants to be a children's book writer and illustrator. Jessi, on the other hand, is passionate about ballet. She wants to be a prima ballerina some day. She takes special ballet lessons in Stamford and has already danced the lead in several productions. Other differences? Mallory's from a huge family and Jessi's from a smaller one. Jessi has two parents, one little sister Becca, one baby brother Squirt (whose real name is John Philip Ramsey, Jr), and her aunt Cecelia. Also, Jessi's black and Mallory's white. That's fine with them and with everyone else, but when Jessi first moved to Stoneybrook, some people in Stoneybrook minded.

Sad. And disgusting.

Our associate club members are Logan Bruno and Shannon Kilbourne.

Logan is Mary Anne's friend *and* boyfriend. Logan's a southerner, and Mary Anne thinks he looks just like her favourite film star, Cam Geary. I admit, Logan *is* cute. And nice. And a good athlete and a good babysitter. He's pretty special, which is the only kind of boy that would be right for Mary Anne. You want the best for your friends, after all.

Shannon Kilbourne is Kristy's neighbour and the person who gave Shannon-the-puppy to the Brewer-Thomas family. And yes, Shannon-the-puppy is named after Shannon Kilbourne. At first Kristy thought Shannon was an awful snob, and Shannon didn't think too much of Kristy, but they settled that and have become friends. Shannon goes to a different school, and is pretty busy (although she comes to some of our meetings, and we're getting to know her better), but she's a good BSC associate. I'm glad she's there in a pinch . . .

"Claud? Claudia, are you there?"

"Oh! Um . . ." Daydreaming at the BSC meeting. This was really bad.

"Subs," prompted Stacey.

"Right," I said. I handed my money over and Stacey put a tick on some account she was keeping.

Kristy finished arranging a sitting date for Dawn, and Mary Anne entered that in the record book, which is where Mary Anne keeps track of all our schedules: our appointments, our jobs, and our after-school activities, so we can tell right away who's free for what job. And please, don't confuse the record book with the club notebook. The notebook is where we write about our various jobs: who our clients are, what happened, how we handled whatever happened, and anything else we think might help us be better babysitters. We're supposed to read the notebook as well as write in it.

Kristy coughed up her subs and the phone rang again.

"Babysitters Club," said Kristy.

"It's Mrs Rodowsky," she told us, after she'd noted the information and told Mrs Rodowsky she'd call her back to tell her who would be taking the job. "You know, Shea's

22

been having trouble at school lately." (We nodded—we'd read the club notebook.)

"Well, they've done some tests and found out he has a reading disorder called dyslexia. So . . ."

"The resource room," I blurted out. "Poor Shea! I bet he has to go to the resource room."

Kristy gave me an odd look and Mary Anne said reasonably, "It's not so bad, Claudia. It's probably a lot better than Shea thinking he's just plain stupid. Now he knows what the problem is and how to work to solve it."

"Yes, but people think you're stupid anyway," I argued.

"Shea's not stupid," said Dawn gently. "Just the opposite, I'd say."

"And he's lucky he *can* learn," said Kristy with surprising vehemence. Then I realized why she was so vehement. She'd babysat for a while for a little girl named Susan, who was autistic. That meant that Susan would probably never change, that she'd always be a withdrawn kid who didn't make contact with other people. Susan was a brilliant pianist, but the rest of the time she was locked inside herself, as if other people didn't even exist.

Kristy had tried to reach Susan. But all her determination and great ideas couldn't change what couldn't be changed.

"Yeah," I said. "I suppose so."

"Anyway, Claudia," said Kristy, "Shea feels the same way you do, I suppose. Mrs Rodowsky says even though he's getting remedial help at school, he also needs help with his homework. But he's so resistant to adults right now that she thought maybe she could hire us to help him from time to time, since we're nearer his age. Or at least, not adults."

"That's not a bad idea," said Stacey thoughtfully. "We had a kids-tutoring-kids programme like that in my school in New York. I was going to be a maths tutor if I'd stayed. It was pretty cool, actually."

Jessi nodded. "When I dance, it does help to see someone close to my age working on the same exercises and routines, for some reason. It's not as intimidating, I suppose."

"Mrs Rodowsky would like to try out her idea starting this Wednesday afternoon," Kristy went on.

Mary Anne ran her finger down the pages of the record book. "Claudia and I are both available."

"Count me out on tutoring, you lot," I said. I didn't add that I was practically in the resource room myself.

"You're sure? Okay." Carefully, Mary Anne entered her name in the book. (Did I mention that she has never, ever made a mistake in the records?)

Stacey zeroed in on me. "Why not, Claudia? You did okay with Rosie Wilder." (She was referring to a babysitting client of ours who was a genius, and had made me feel amazingly stupid—until I realized that underneath she was as human as the rest of us, and that what she really wanted was not to be a genius-at-large, but an artist. *That* I could help her with.)

I sighed. I should have known my best friend would sense that things weren't going too well for me. "Why not? Well, this is the deal. Mrs Hall told me that if I don't get a good grade, a really good grade, in the English test coming up two weeks from Wednesday, I'm going to fail English."

"Oh, no!" gasped Mary Anne.

"You need to get some help," said Kristy briskly.

"No kidding," I said, depression washing over me. "Especially since a big part of the test is going to be spelling and vocabulary."

"How about the resource room?" said Dawn neutrally.

"No! I mean, I don't have to go, yet. But if I don't pass this test . . ."

"Wait a minute!" Stacey leaned forward. "What about us?"

"I don't know," I said. "What about you?"

"Tutoring you! We're tutoring Shea. Why couldn't we tutor you?"

"Practice," said Jessi. "She's right. What you need is practice!"

See what I mean? Friends. I didn't get a lump in my throat, but it really meant a lot, and I said so.

Kristy waved her hand as if to brush all that sentimentality aside. "What about it, Claudia? Are you going to let us tutor you?"

"I'd like to. Let me check with my parents and let you know after dinner."

"Okay," said Kristy. She looked at her watch. "Oh, lord. It's nearly six o'clock! I'd better call Mrs Rodowsky back."

Shea was a lucky kid to have the Babysitters Club on his side, I thought, relaxing and letting my thoughts drift. And so, for that matter, was I.

3rd
CHAPTER

"Ahem!" I said.

Neither of my parents, who were sitting at the kitchen table drinking coffee, looked up.

It was after dinner. I'd decided to be responsible and mature about the English test and talk to my parents as soon as the time was right. Of course, the time never seems right to give people, especially parents, bad news. But some times are better than others. For instance, I didn't bring up the subject at the dinner table with my sister the genius there. Janine isn't unkind, but she's not exactly sensitive the way Mary Anne is either.

I closed my eyes for a minute and imagined the scene. Janine would finish talking about brussels sprouts as a cruciferous vegetable. (I *think* that means they're

27

definitely not junk food. Whatever they are, they aren't my favourites.) Anyway, I'd mention, casually, that I was having a little trouble in English. My father, who's a partner in an investment firm and a fanatic about accuracy, would say immediately: "Define what you mean by 'a little trouble', Claudia." So I'd begin explaining and my mother, who's head librarian at the Stoney-brook library and therefore very good at English, would look puzzled and then serious. How could she have a daughter who didn't love school? Especially English?

Then Janine, who doesn't understand how someone can even get a "B" in a subject, much less be in danger of failing, would say, "Your mental capacities, Claudia, are more than adequate to surmount any difficulties in the average middle school subjects. Are you addressing yourself to the subject in question as you should?"

Which would mean, "Claudia, you're not stupid. So you can't be trying."

Unfortunately, Janine would only be saying what my parents and teachers and everybody believes: that I'm an under-achiever.

They don't understand how hard it is not to be bored out of my mind by school. I don't understand it myself.

"Claudia?"

I opened my eyes. Both my parents were looking at me.

"Oh! Hi."

"Hello, Claudia," said my mother. She smiled.

"I've got to talk to you," I blurted out.

My mother patted the seat of the chair next to her, still smiling a little. "Sit down then. Would you like something to drink?"

"Milk," I said quickly. "I'll just pour myself a glass of milk." Having a glass of milk in my hand gave me something to hold on to.

With the glass of milk clutched in my hand, I sat down.

"Well, Claudia?" asked my father.

I took a gulp of milk. "The good news is I'm not failing English . . ."

My parents waited.

". . . yet," I finished weakly.

The little smile left my mother's face. But she said calmly, "Perhaps you'd better explain a little more."

So I did. I told them about the conversation with Mrs Hall, and about the conversation with my friends in the BSC.

"So," I concluded. "I can study really hard, and with the help of my friends, I feel I can handle the test."

I stopped and suddenly realized I had a

milk moustache. So much for looking mature and responsible. I quickly wiped it off while my parents had a conversation with their eyes (you know how parents do that).

Finally my mother said, "It does sound as though you've thought this through. We're willing to let you handle it in your own way."

"Oh, good!"

"But there are conditions."

Uh-oh! I started to take another nervous gulp of milk, then realized I'd finished the whole glass.

"We'll talk to Mrs Hall and find out what material the test will cover. Someone will continue to check your homework every night." (I forgot to mention this is one of the rules in our house.) "And we will also periodically check on the work you are doing on your own and with your friends. Is that a deal?"

"It's a deal," I said happily. I stood up, rinsed the glass, and put it in the sink. "Thank you, *thank you*," I said.

"Don't thank us. It's up to you," my father reminded me.

"I know. I have to phone everyone and tell them," I said. I added quickly, "And arrange tutoring dates."

My father's eyes twinkled a little, I think.

"Yes," he said. "You'd better do that."

I've tutored people before. I'm the one who taught Emily Michelle her shapes and colours. And I've been tutored, of course, in the resource room. But I've never been tutored by someone who's my own age *and* my friend. Particularly my best friend.

So I'm not sure what I expected the next afternoon at my first tutoring session with Stacey. One thing I wasn't expecting was that she would be so strict. She came over to my house right after school. I was trying to clear up my room. (It's usually a little—well, a lot—messy.) But I'd got sidetracked by the discovery of a package of gourmet coconut macadamia nut biscuits, and was finishing one off when Stacey came into the room.

"Pretzels?" I said, offering her a bag of sourdough pretzels.

"No, thank you," said Stacey.

"Where do you want to sit?" I asked. "I've cleared my bed. But I can move all the junk that's on my desk to the floor. Or we can work on the floor."

Stacey shook her head. "No."

"No? No, we're not going to work? No, you've changed your mind?" I grabbed my hair and pretended to pull it out in horror.

Stacey didn't even smile. "No, we're not going to work on your bed or on the floor or

31

at the desk. We're not going to work in your room."

"We're not?"

"Where's your English book? Please get it, your notebook, and whatever else you need and come with me."

Mystified, I did what Stacey told me and followed her meekly down the stairs to the kitchen.

"Good. No one's around." Stacey went over to the table and pulled out a chair. "You sit here."

I sat. I watched in amazement as Stacey cleared the kitchen table, unplugged the telephone, and turned the clock radio so it faced the wall and I couldn't see what time it was.

"You've forgotten the timer clock on the oven," I pointed out. "I can still see that."

Even my sarcasm didn't throw Stacey. She shifted a saucepan so it was in front of the oven clock. Then, hands on her hips, she surveyed the rest of the kitchen with a little frown.

"Okay," she said finally.

She sat down next to me and pulled the books towards her.

"Er, Stace? What are we doing in the kitchen, exactly?"

"We're here because there are too many distractions in your room. And what I just did, as I think you guessed by your little comment about the oven clock, was to remove all distractions here in the kitchen."

"Gosh, Stacey, we're going to study! Not write a Newbery award winner."

Stacey raised her eyebrows. (She looked very New York, if you know what I mean.) "This is just as important," she said. "Or it should be, to you."

Wow! I didn't know what to say. It didn't matter. Stacey obviously wasn't expecting me to disagree.

Stacey flipped open the English book. "Use the following words as modifiers in a complete sentence," she read aloud.

I won't say time went by quickly. I personally think it's twice as hard to study without a clock to watch. And I personally was sick of the "following words" as modifiers or as anything else by the time we finished my homework. But Stacey wasn't.

I admit it, my mouth dropped open when she pulled a bundle of index cards out of her bag.

"What are those?" I said.

"Flash cards," she announced. "Or they will be."

"Flash cards. Like little kids use?"

"Like anybody uses to help with her spelling," Stacey told me. "Here. Write each word on a card and we'll go through them a few times."

"A few times?" I said. My voice rose.

"Claudia, do you want to pass this test, or don't you?"

I sighed a little sigh. I looked around the kitchen. No clocks. No radios. No telephones. It was like a weird art piece. I wondered if I could do something with it somehow. Maybe . . .

"Claudia!"

I pulled the cards towards me and began to write.

My father got home just as we were finishing.

"Hello Stacey, Claudia. Working hard?"

"Yes," I said. I tried not to sound glum about it.

"Good," said my father. He disappeared in the direction of the family room and I looked at the stack of cards.

"Again?" I said.

"No, that's enough for today," replied Stacey. "You don't want to be too tired to do your other homework."

"Gee, thanks," I said.

Folding her arms, Stacey gave me a Look.

"Claudia, this is serious. Do you remember what happened the last time your schoolwork took a slide? Do you?"

"I guess so," I said.

"Like your parents saying you'd have to give up the Babysitters Club?"

"I know." I felt guilty then, for giving Stacey any trouble at all. "I'm sorry, Stace. I don't know. Somehow complaining seems to make things easier."

Stacey's face relaxed into a grin. She began gathering up her notebooks and books and pens. "I know, I know. Kvetching."

"Kvetching?"

"It's Yiddish. And New Yorkish . . . it means complaining as an art form."

"Kvetching." I tried the word out again. It sounded just like what it was. "I like that."

"I have to go," Stacey said.

"Thanks a lot, Stace. I really appreciate this."

"Until next time, then."

"Until next time," I echoed.

"Right. Meanwhile, keep going over those words."

"Yes, ma'am!" I said.

I walked Stacey to the door, then went back to my room. My brain felt like porridge, but I'd had an idea about those flash cards. If I had to look at them over and over again, at least I could make them better to look at. In my room, I cleared my desk, then spread the cards out on one side of it and my coloured pencils on the other.

"Embarrass" was the first card. That was easy. The card deserved a red theme because when I get embarrassed my face turns red.

By the time dinner was ready, I'd decorated most of the vocabulary cards with the coloured pencils. I was actually enjoying myself.

I must have looked pretty pleased when I sat down at the table. Janine finished unfolding her napkin and then said to me, "You appear to be in remarkably salubrious spirits, considering your situation."

"Are you talking about the tutoring?" I asked.

"I was referring to your coursework review, yes."

"Oh, I'm not kvetching," I said airily.

Janine's eyes widened, and I burst out laughing.

I decided I'd better ask Stacey how to spell "kvetching". It was probably my new favourite word.

4th CHAPTER

Wednesday

It was a little strange to be at the Rodowskys' and not keep an eye on Jackie and Archie while I was with Shea. But I forgot about that pretty quickly. I was worried about Shea. I think he's given up. I still don't understand exactly what being dyslexic must mean for him, but I do understand that it must be very, very frustrating. I think, though, that Shea is more than frustrated. I think he really thinks he is dumb...

After school on Wednesday Mary Anne reached the Rodowskys' as soon as she could, which meant she was a little early. She wanted to make sure she had a chance to talk to Mrs Rodowsky first. It was a good thing she did give herself that extra time, because Mrs Rodowksy had quite a bit she wanted to tell Mary Anne.

They went into the family room and Mrs Rodowsky closed the door behind her.

"I want to explain to you what Shea has been through," she told Mary Anne.

Mary Anne was relieved. She had a lot of questions, but she wasn't quite sure where to start. She was glad Mrs Rodowsky was going to begin.

Folding her hands in her lap, Mrs Rodowsky said, "Shea has always had trouble in school. But just recently we realized that he might have a specific learning disorder. When we did realize that, Shea had to undergo a number of tests to determine if that was the problem."

"What kind of tests?" asked Mary Anne.

"He's been evaluated by neurologists, eye doctors, hearing specialists, reading disorder specialists, reading disorder counsellors and special educators. A number of things had to be ruled out, you see."

"Oh," said Mary Anne.

"Once we had ruled out all the other possibilities, we realized that what Shea has is dyslexia. You may have heard of that before."

"I have, but I'm not sure what it means."

"It's a pretty broad term. In Shea's case, it means he has problems recognizing letters and words, and sometimes numbers, on the printed page. He reverses letters, like 'b' for 'd' and words like 'was' for 'saw'. He might see a '6' as a '9'. Very young children do this when they're just learning to read. But for some children, it persists even when they're older."

Mary Anne said thoughtfully, "Shea must have had to work twice as hard, just to keep up."

Mrs Rodowsky leaned forward and put her hand on Mary Anne's. "Yes!" she said. "In a lot of ways, he's had to be twice as clever. Unfortunately, he doesn't feel that way. The tests show Shea has above average intelligence. But with all these tests and tutoring, he's convinced himself he's just the opposite. He . . . he calls himself a 'dummy'."

"But he's not," said Mary Anne.

"That's where I'm hoping you can help. You're closer to Shea in age. Maybe he won't feel so pressured if he's working with you. He's so suspicious now of us adults and all our tests . . ." Mrs Rodowsky shook her head. "Maybe you can help."

An enormous crash from the kitchen brought both Mrs Rodowsky and Mary Anne to their feet.

"Jackie!" exclaimed Mary Anne. Then she looked quickly at Mrs Rodowsky, hoping she hadn't hurt her feelings by assuming the crash had been caused by Jackie (also known among his babysitters as the Walking Disaster).

But Mrs Rodowsky wasn't upset. "Jackie," she agreed. "Shea's in his room. Why don't you join him?"

So instead of hurrying to see what Jackie had crashed into, knocked down, fallen on, or tripped over, Mary Anne went to Shea's room.

Shea was hunched over his desk, his hands clenched into fists and dug into his cheeks. Lopsided stacks of books and ragged-edged piles of papers covered the surface. Shea wasn't looking at them, though. He was staring out of the window above the desk.

Mary Anne stepped inside the open door and said, "Shea?"

Shea half turned his head without moving the rest of his body. "Yeah?"

"It's me. Mary Anne."

"Hi, Mary Anne." Shea didn't sound very enthusiastic.

Mary Anne walked into the room and said, "Do you mind if I pull up a chair?"

"Okay," said Shea. His level of enthusiasm didn't change.

"What are you working on?" asked Mary Anne.

Shea unclenched his fists and waved his hands, as if he wanted to shoo the question away. "Homework."

"What homework? Maths? Geography? English?"

Shea made the same gesture, with an added sort of hopelessness to it. "I dunno."

"Okay. Why don't you see what your homework is, and then decide what you want to work on?"

"That's what Mrs Danvers said I should do," Shea said. "She's my teacher. She said I should make a list of my homework assignments and the books I'll need."

Mary Anne nodded. "Sometimes even making a list is a pain, but that sounds like a good idea." She eyed the chaos on his desk and said, "Okay, for a start, what *are* your subjects in school?"

Shea told Mary Anne what his subjects were. Then they made a list of the subjects for which Shea had homework assignments that night. Next to each assignment, they wrote down everything Shea would need for it: books, notebooks, notes, pens, pencils, paper, whatever.

Then, finally, they started on the homework.

"For English," Mary Anne said, studying the list, "you're supposed to write a letter to someone you admire."

Shea frowned.

"*Anybody* you admire," said Mary Anne. "Who's your favourite . . . athlete?"

Shea shrugged. Then he said, "I like Jackie Robinson. He was a hero."

"I think Jackie Robinson is, er, dead, Shea."

"My teacher didn't say we had to write to a live person."

"True," said Mary Anne. "Okay, why don't you write to Jackie Robinson. What do you need?"

"A pencil and some paper," said Shea, grabbing his pencil and pulling a sheet of paper towards him. "First we write our name and address and the date in the right-hand corner."

He bent his head, started to write in the left corner, rubbed it out, moved to the right, then back to the left, and finally settled on the right. He wrote laboriously. "Then we write the person's name and address below that." He wrote for a minute longer, then said, "What address do I use for Jackie Robinson?"

Where do you send a letter to a dead person? Mary Anne wondered. Then she remembered that Jackie Robinson had played for the Dodgers. "You could send it care of the Dodgers. In Los Angeles," she suggested.

"Okay."

For a long time after that the room was quiet as Shea wrote and rubbed out and wrote some more. Finally he looked up. "Here," he said. He handed Mary Anne his letter.

Daer Jackie Rodinson,
    Your my favorite baseball player. You are so very very goob. The best. I nevir got to sea you play, but I have sen picshures fo you and movise, to. You where brave. You fouhgt prejubis and played baseball to. You could do anything you wanted do to. You are a world famuos person and a heroe.
                Your admirer,
                Shae Rodowsky
P.S. My bor there's name is Jackie, to.

"It's a good letter, Shea," Mary Anne said. "But I think it needs a little more work."

Shea threw down his pencil. "It's all wrong, isn't it? I can't do anything right."

"That's not true," began Mary Anne.

"It is, too," said Shea. "I'm stupid and daft and dopey."

"No, you're not!"

Shea didn't look convinced. "If I'm not, how come my letter's not right?"

"Nobody's perfect," said Mary Anne. "You're better at some things than others, so you have to work harder on some things."

"I'm dyslexic," said Shea bitterly. "That means I'm stupid."

"It means you learn things differently from most other people. It doesn't mean you're stupid."

Shea folded his arms and scowled.

"Come on," said Mary Anne. "We'll make this letter perfect. But to make something perfect, you have to make some changes, sometimes. Mostly you just need to sort out your spelling."

At last Mary Anne persuaded Shea to work on the letter. And bit by bit, he got it right.

A funny thing happened while they were working, though. Mary Anne kept getting the feeling she was being watched. And sure enough, once when she turned around, Jackie and Archie were standing in the doorway of Shea's room.

"Hello," said Mary Anne.

"Hi," said Jackie.

"We're working right now," Mary Anne told them.

"We know," said Jackie, grinning.

Mary Anne turned back to Shea.

A few minutes later she looked over her shoulder. Jackie and Archie were still there. Jackie leaned over and whispered something to Archie and they both grinned.

Were they laughing at Shea? Mary Anne didn't think so. Jackie was a Walking Disaster, but he was a good person.

"Jackie, Archie? Can I do something for you?"

"No," said Archie.

"No," said Jackie. They both just kept grinning.

"Fine, we'll keep working then." Mary Anne turned back to the desk again. A moment later she turned around. Jackie and Archie were *still* there.

"Goodbye," said Mary Anne firmly.

"Oh!" said Jackie. "Goodbye."

"'Bye," said Archie.

Reluctantly, the two of them slid away. A few minutes later she heard Archie shriek, "Look out!" from the back of the house and she knew he and Jackie had found something else to occupy them.

Mary Anne decided the boys must have been jealous because Shea had her undivided attention. Or maybe they were confused because Mary Anne had switched from babysitter to tutor.

"It's a good letter," said Mary Anne at last. It was a little smudged, but spellingwise, it was perfect. "An excellent letter."

Shea took it and carefully put it beneath the pages of his English notebook. "I suppose so."

Looking at her watch, Mary Anne said, "Uh-oh! I'd better go. It's almost time for my Babysitters Club meeting."

She thought Shea would ask her questions about the meeting, or say something. But he didn't.

His head sank on to his fists. He stared out of the window. "Okay," he said.

"You did some good work, Shea."

"Yeah."

Mary Anne paused. She didn't know what else to say. "Well, 'bye," she said at last.

"Goodbye," said Shea softly. He sounded as discouraged and sad as he looked.

5th CHAPTER

"Babysitters Club," Jessi answered the phone crisply. She wedged the receiver between her ear and her shoulder, grabbed a pencil with one hand and her notebook with the other, and began to scribble down information.

It was Wednesday afternoon and business as usual. In fact, maybe a little more business than usual.

I'd already taken one job, and that was all I was going to allow myself with the test coming up. Jessi hung up and I watched as Mary Anne flipped through the book to schedule the appointment.

"You can just write down 'studying' for me for every afternoon, evening and weekend," I said mournfully.

"In between your art lessons and the BSC meetings?" asked Mary Anne innocently.

Mallory gave me a jab with her elbow and I grimaced. Mary Anne finished logging in the latest job and then said, "You know, I was with Shea Rodowsky this afternoon."

"That's right," said Jessi. "How did that go?"

Mary Anne grimaced. "I'm not really sure. I talked to Mrs Rodowsky first and she explained more about dyslexia."

"You know, I've just remembered something," said Dawn. "A friend of mine in California has got dyslexia. I remember she was really brainy. She could understand how *anything* worked. But she had trouble reading basic instructions."

"What happened to her?" asked Kristy.

"Nothing." Dawn looked surprised. "She took some special classes for a while, and she started tape recording all her usual classes because she took notes so slowly. She was building a sailing boat when I left. Said she was going to finish it in time for high school graduation, then sail around the world."

"I wish Shea could meet your friend, Dawn," said Mary Anne. "He thinks he's stupid and hopeless and daft. Dopey, that's what he called himself."

"Shea's not stupid!" said Stacey indignantly. "Anybody who's spent any time with him would know that."

"That's right. In fact, his mother told me he has above average intelligence."

"What *does* dyslexia mean, anyway?" asked Mallory.

"It's a learning disability, or learning difference," Mary Anne replied. "A dyslexic person doesn't see things the same way other people do. He reverses letters or words. He might read 'was' for 'saw'. He doesn't even know he's doing it. He just knows he's not keeping up with everyone else in his class. So he thinks he's stupid."

"Wow! Scary!" said Mallory.

"It must be, rather," said Mary Anne.

"But now that the Rodowskys know what the problem is, they can deal with it, right?" That was Kristy, of course.

"I'm not sure it's that easy," Mary Anne replied.

"I didn't mean it was easy," said Kristy. "I just meant that they've got a solution to the problem."

"Yes. But knowing what the problem is, and knowing how to correct it, isn't making Shea feel any better. And I'm not sure what we can do."

"Give him lots of praise and encouragement," suggested Jessi.

Mary Anne nodded. "That's a good idea. But it has to be genuine, or Shea's going to think we're just trying to make him feel better."

"True," said Kristy. "And that would be even worse."

"Like when you give a really lousy dance performance," Jessi said, "and everyone says how wonderful you are. You feel fifty times worse than if someone said something a little more truthful . . ."

"Like you were awful?" Mallory raised her eyebrows at Jessi.

"No! Just something more truthful. I don't know. Like, this part of the performance looked good, but that part needed work."

"It depends on who's saying it, too, don't you think?" asked Dawn.

Mary Anne said, "But what about . . ."

As you may have noticed, I pretty much stayed out of this discussion. I'd heard the word dyslexia before, too. It was one of the words that had come up in conversations between my parents and my teachers in the past when I started doing not-so-well in school. A long, long time ago, they had even tested me for learning disabilities. It turned out I didn't have any learning disabilities, and that I was supposed to be brighter than your average kid. Which hadn't made my parents or me too happy. Now they had proof I was a plain old under-achiever, which meant they'd never leave me alone.

On the other hand, I don't like feeling stupid, which is the way I feel compared with my genius sister sometimes. I was glad to know I wasn't really stupid. I just didn't like school. Of course, I could go to one of those schools to study special things, like that high school in the film *Fame* where the kids learn to be dancers and performers and artists. A school like that would be okay . . .

"Claudia, you know, this reminds me, you need to schedule another tutoring session." Stacey was looking over Mary Anne's shoulder at the book.

"Right." I tried to look as if I'd been listening.

Stacey ran her finger down the page. "Here. Here's a good time for me, and you're free."

"You're pretty booked up that week, Stace," I said. "Are you sure you don't want someone else to take me on?"

"No. You know I want to be your tutor. Your *only* tutor. I think it'd be more effective and less confusing that way. What do you think?"

"Er . . ." I said.

Kristy said, "Are you sure, Stacey?"

"Positive." Stacey gave me a big smile.

I couldn't help but smile back. Stacey was a true best friend.

"It's fine with me if it's fine with everybody else." Kristy looked around and the others nodded.

"Done," said Stacey.

"Gimme five!" I said. We were right in the middle of a really stupid high five routine that looked like a bad cheer when a knock sounded on the door.

Mallory opened it and said, "Hi, Janine."

"Hello," said Janine. "Claudia, I arrived home a few minutes ago to find this affixed to the front door."

Janine held out an envelope with the letters "BSC" printed across it.

"BSC being the abbreviation for the Babysitters Club, I naturally assumed it was directed to you."

"Gosh, thanks Janine." I took the envelope and ripped it open. Inside on a plain piece of white paper was a typewritten message: YOU ARE VERY NICE.

I held it up.

Janine pushed up her glasses. "It would appear to be the work of an anonymous admirer. How gratifying."

"Thanks," I said.

"You're quite welcome," she said as she left.

"Who's it for?" asked Kristy.

I shook my head. "Doesn't say."

"Well, who is it from?" asked Jessi.

I turned the paper and the envelope over. "Doesn't say that either. Like Janine said, it's anonymous."

"It's a very sweet note," said Mary Anne.

"Yeah," I said.

"This isn't really something Bart would do," said Kristy thoughtfully. "He's pretty straightforward. But . . ."

"What a lovely thing for *Logan* to do." Mary Anne's eyes filled with tears. She reached one hand up to touch the little pearl earrings that Logan had bought at the SMS auction and given to her.

"Hey," said Mallory. "Logan gives you earrings. He doesn't have to send you an anonymous note. I bet it's from Ben. It's hard for him to say things like that to me. It's probably much easier to write it anonymously."

I looked around the room and realized we'd all decided that the mystery note was from a particular boy, and meant just for one of us. And why not? I admit, I was sort of hoping it was from Austin Bentley, a boy at school who is on my top ten cute guys list. I was about to blurt that out when Kristy said thoughtfully, "Remember those notes that Cokie and Grace sent me that time?"

"Your 'mystery admirer'," said Stacey. "That was a pretty disgusting trick."

"Pretty typical for them, though," pointed out Dawn.

"They wouldn't do it again, though," argued Mary Anne. "It would be stupid to try the same trick twice."

Dawn shook her head. "They might just be stupid enough to try it."

"To see if we're stupid enough to fall for it," said Kristy.

"No way!" said Jessi. "Come on, you don't really believe they'd do that again."

"Maybe not," said Mary Anne. "It is a pretty sweet note. Not Cokie's or Grace's style."

"True," said Kristy.

"Maybe . . . maybe it's got something to do with the Spring Dance at the Community Centre!" exclaimed Dawn.

"Yes!" cried Mallory. Then she hesitated. "But what?"

"I don't know. Something. Some guy we haven't even thought of as a possibility maybe, just sort of testing the waters."

"Oooh," said Mary Anne dreamily. "How romantic."

"Yeah," said Jessi, her voice trailing off.

We were quiet for just a second, trying to imagine this dream guy. Then Kristy looked at her watch.

"Whoa! It's after six o'clock. I bet Charlie's downstairs waiting for me!" Kristy jumped to her feet and grabbed her rucksack. "This meeting of the BSC is officially adjourned," she announced and raced out of the door.

Everyone stood up slowly and followed her. Our thoughts were far away.

As for me, I folded the note carefully, and put it in my jewellery box.

6th
CHAPTER

I had only taken on one new babysitting job since Mrs Hall dropped her bombshell on me, but I had already scheduled one for Friday afternoon at the Rodowskys'. It was a regular sitting job for Jackie, Archie and Shea, of course, not a tutoring session (phew!), so I put on my usual jeans and a big old shirt. It's my spill-proof, accident-proof outfit, and when you babysit for Jackie, who in addition to being the Walking Disaster is one of three very active brothers, that kind of fashion planning is essential.

"The boys are in the garden playing ball," Mrs Rodowsky told me when I arrived. "Chocolate chip and oatmeal raisin biscuits are in the biscuit barrel in the kitchen, for snacktime." There's another reason I like sitting for the Rodowskys. Mrs Rodowsky always has something good to eat on hand—something not *too* healthy.

She picked her carrier bag up from the kitchen chair. "I'm taking the car for a quick oil change, and then I'm going to run errands. Here's a list of places I'll be. You know where the usual emergency numbers and so on are."

I nodded.

"You know about Shea?" she asked.

I nodded again and said, "He's got dyslexia."

She smiled a little. "It's good to know what the problem is. Now that we do, we're working on it." (Almost exactly what Kristy had said!)

Mrs Rodowsky paused. "We're working on it," she repeated. "But Shea's suffering from lack of self-esteem. This isn't a tutoring session, but anything you can say to encourage him would be helpful."

"I'll remember," I promised.

Mrs Rodowsky grinned. "Good. See you in an hour and a half."

After she left, I went out to the garden. It isn't a big garden because of the dog-kennel and a toolshed. Fortunately, the toolshed doesn't have any windows, so the hitting and pitching practice wasn't too hazardous. Still, I noticed that Bo, the Rodowskys' dog, was busily working on a bone *behind* his kennel, keeping one eye cocked towards the rest of his family.

"Hi, guys!" I said.

"Hi!" called Jackie. He looked up and grinned a big gap-toothed grin—and the ball sailed past him to land on the roof of Bo's kennel. Bo flattened his ears and rolled his eyes as the ball bounced down the roof and landed with a thump on the ground.

"Oops!" said Jackie.

"Concentrate!" admonished Shea.

I should mention that the Rodowsky boys love softball. Jackie plays on a softball team, Kristy's Krushers, coached by none other than our fearless Babysitters Club chairman. You have to be pretty fearless to coach this team, since the average age of the players is 5.8 years. It was another one of Kristy's great ideas, when she realized that there were no teams for such a, well, age-diversified group of kids who weren't exactly Little League material. As a player, Jackie's something of a threat, not only because you might say that the element of surprise is always on his side, but also because he's a pretty solid hitter. He once even hit a home run.

And although Archie, who's four, isn't a Krusher (at least not yet) or a power hitter or much of an outfielder, you can tell he gets a big kick out of the game. And he's a pretty good athlete. He goes to gym classes and plays for a *very* junior soccer team, too.

Shea isn't a Krusher. He's in the Little League. He's an excellent player, and he isn't conceited about it, either. Right now, he was pitching slow, careful pitches to Archie so that Archie could hit them. And every time Archie did, even if the ball just brushed the bat, Shea would say, "that's the idea" or "you got a little wood on it that time." He was patient, too, about fielding Jackie's throws back to him. (Jackie was the catcher.)

"Do you want to play, Claudia?" asked Jackie.

"I could catch," I said. "You and Archie could take turns batting."

Jackie thought it was a great idea, so a few minutes later I was crouching behind first Archie, then Jackie, wearing Shea's batting helmet just in case. Archie got some nice bunts and Jackie got one outstanding hit—right against the wall of the toolshed.

Shea pushed his cap back. "Too bad that shed was in the way, Jackie. I think you would have hit a home run."

"Really? Oh, wow! Pow, pow, pow!" Jackie took a few celebratory swings with his bat, wound himself up too tight, and toppled over.

"How about some catching practice?" I

suggested. "We've got two balls—"

"I'll throw to Archie and you throw to Shea," said Jackie.

"Okay." We settled into a nice groove, punctuated by the slap, slap of the balls hitting the gloves. But then I noticed that Jackie and Archie were edging closer and closer together.

A minute later, they were whispering to one another. Then Jackie announced, "I'm tired. Can we stop now?"

I looked at Shea, who shrugged.

"Okay. It's not quite time for snacks, yet, though," I said.

"That's okay. We've got a project to work on," replied Jackie.

We trailed back into the house and put the equipment away in the cupboard in the playroom. Then Jackie and Archie, still whispering, ran upstairs to Jackie's room and shut the door.

"They must have something important to do," I commented. "What about you, Shea?"

Shea ran his hand along the edge of a chair. "Nothing."

"You're doing some new stuff at school, aren't you? How's that going?"

"Fine."

"Are you studying anything interesting? Anything you like?"

Shea shrugged. Then he pulled the chair out and sat down at the playroom table, which was covered with art supplies.

"Do you like art? I *love* art. It's probably my best subject. In fact, I like it so much, I don't even count it as a subject."

Shea smiled a little then and reached for a half-finished painting. His hand brushed a small container of paint. The lid was just resting on top, not screwed on tightly, and the paint spilled across the table.

"Oops!" I said. I grabbed a roll of paper towels, handed some to Shea, and we began to blot up the paint.

"What an idiot! What an idiot!" Shea muttered.

"Shea? What are you talking about? You're not an idiot."

"Yes, I am. I'm stupid at school. Something's wrong with me."

Mary Anne was right. Shea was upset. I took a deep breath—and chickened out.

I didn't say what I really wanted to say. Instead I said, "Shea, there's nothing wrong with you. You just learn things a different way. Now that you know that and what to do about it, you can work hard and concentrate. Remember, like you told Jackie? Concentrate. You can do it. Just pay attention and try your best."

Blah, blah, blah! I didn't sound very

convincing. The words had a familiar ring (I'd heard them a thousand times before from my parents and teachers). I certainly don't think I convinced Shea.

He threw down the paper towels and pushed away the painting.

"Well, tired of art, huh?" I said brightly. "Listen, have you got any homework? Why don't I help you with that?"

"I don't know," said Shea.

"Let's give it a try. It can't hurt." Shea nodded. "Come on, then." We went to his room.

The top of Shea's desk wasn't quite as chaotic as I'd expected. In fact, after I'd pulled up a chair next to him, I realized that each pile was for a specific thing: maths, social sciences, earth sciences. I think Shea was beginning to make progress, whether he believed it or not.

"Where do you want to begin?" I asked. I looked over the desk. "I know. How about science? What are you doing in science?" (I couldn't face the thought of helping him with maths.)

"We're supposed to make a list of ten things that will help the environment, and then explain why," said Shea. He sighed and pulled a book towards him.

"What a great idea! Have you read the

chapter?" I leaned over and studied the first page.

"Listen, here's a great idea: put a time switch on your hot water tank."

Shea didn't say anything.

"Why don't you write that down," I said.

Reluctantly, he picked up the pencil and wrote:

> Qut a timer no the hot watter tack.

"Good, that's a good start. But look at the first word, Shea. It's not quite right."

"It wouldn't be," muttered Shea.

"It's nothing much. Look." I picked up a pencil and on a separate sheet of paper wrote "Put". "See?"

Shea stared at what I'd written for several seconds, his brows furrowed. Then he said, "Oh." He rubbed out the back-to-front "P" and substituted the correct one. Then he wrote:

> Use laevs and gras clippings no your lane and flower deb.

"Shea, wait. We haven't finished the first one yet."

Shea frowned. "Yes, we have. I've corrected the P."

63

"But there are a couple of other things. Just a couple."

Shea put his pencil down. "I don't want to do this any more."

"Come on, Shea. Keep trying. Come on!"

Frowning even harder, Shea picked up his pencil.

"Now," I said. "In the first sentence, you wrote 'no' for 'on'."

"I didn't," said Shea. He paused and stared at the sentence. "I . . . I did."

"Just reverse the letters," I said. "See?"

Painstakingly, Shea began to rub out the word and rewrite the letters.

I heard a whisper behind me.

Sure enough, Archie and Jackie were standing in the doorway, looking serious.

"Okay, you two, what is it? Have you finished your project?"

"Our project? Nooo. Not yet," answered Jackie.

"Do you need me to do something?"

"Uh-uh." Archie shook his head.

Then Jackie grinned. "'Bye," he said.

Giggling, he and Archie ducked out of sight.

What was that all about? I wondered. Then I remembered that the same thing had happened to Mary Anne. *Were* Archie and Jackie jealous of the attention Shea was getting? I shook my head. I couldn't tell.

I turned back to Shea. Number 3, he'd written.

"Er, Shea, wait a minute."

"Now what?"

"You still have just a couple more things to correct on number 1."

Suddenly Shea threw his pencil across the room. "I hate this. I hate it! I can't do anything right."

"Shea—"

"No. You can't make me! You're not my teacher."

"Of course not. I was just trying to help."

"Don't help me! I don't need any help. You can't help an *idiot*!"

Before I could answer, I heard Mrs Rodowsky opening the door downstairs and calling, "Boys? Claudia? I'm back."

"Shea," I said.

Ignoring me, Shea slid out of his chair and ran out of the room.

Mrs Rodowsky met me in the hall. "I'm a little early. Snacktime for everybody?"

"Snacks, hooray!" said Jackie. He flung his arms out and hit the edge of the hall table. It teetered, and I made a diving save.

Mrs Rodowsky smiled. "Good work, Claudia. Now let me see, what do I owe you?"

As Mrs Rodowsky paid me and the boys

65

milled around us, I sneaked a quick look at Shea. He didn't look cheered up by the snacks. He didn't look happy at all.

"Thank you, Claudia," said Mrs Rodowsky.

I wanted to say, don't thank me. I think I've just made things worse. But I didn't. I just nodded and smiled and left, feeling useless.

7th
CHAPTER

I was the last one to arrive at the Friday afternoon meeting of the BSC. I felt kind of funny, dashing into my own room and seeing everyone else sitting around.

"You're on time," Kristy told me approvingly.

Then the phone rang.

"Here," said Mallory, passing me a bag of liquorice sticks left over from the last meeting. "I remembered you'd hidden these in your bottom desk drawer."

"Thanks," I said. I took a few to sustain me while I rooted out the bumper pack of M&M's from behind the second shelf of books on my bookcase. Stacey was drinking a diet soda, and Dawn was carefully ignoring all the unhealthy junk food circulating the room.

"You were at the Rodowskys' today,

weren't you?" asked Mary Anne. "How was it?"

"Not good," I admitted.

"What happened, Claud?" asked Stacey.

"It's Shea. You're right, Mary Anne. He thinks he's the world's biggest idiot. He knocked over some paint, and right away he started calling himself stupid. It was just an accident!"

"Oh, poor Shea," said Mary Anne.

"Poor Shea is right," I agreed. "But what can we do about it?"

"We've just started this tutoring stuff," Kristy said. "We need to give that a chance. We can't expect results overnight."

"True," I said.

Then, just like on Wednesday, I heard a knock at the door, and a moment later I was taking an envelope out of Janine's hand.

"I found this attached to the front door when I got home," she said.

"Thanks," I replied.

"That's all right."

As Janine left, I held the envelope up.

Just as before, the letters "BSC" were written on the envelope. I ripped the envelope open and a plain sheet of white paper with typewritten words on it fell out: YOU ARE THE BEST.

"The best what?" said Stacey, who's always precise.

"It's another note from a secret admirer!" Mary Anne's eyes were shining.

"Maybe yes, maybe no," said Kristy. "Don't forget, we've been sent secret notes before, and they *weren't* from secret admirers."

"They didn't sound as genuinely nice, though," said Mary Anne. "I mean, these don't sound fake. Do they?"

"I don't think so," said Dawn.

"Although they are kind of, well, short," said Mallory. "I mean, if I were going to write a note to someone I secretly admired, I'd be more elegant."

"And specific," Jessi said. "We don't even know who this is addressed to."

"We do know it arrived at about the same time of day as the last one, in the same way," Kristy said.

"Do you think someone's watching the house?" I asked. "I was the last one here and I didn't see anybody lurking around or anything. Of course, I wasn't looking, either."

Stacey examined the note. "No clues here," she said. "It could be from a typewriter or a printer . . . Claud, what about Janine? These notes aren't from her, are they?"

I thought for a minute. "Nah. It's not something Janine would do. For one thing, she'd use bigger words, probably. And for another, if this is a joke of some kind, it's not her style."

"I vote it's a secret admirer, just dying to ask one of us to the dance," said Dawn.

"Seconded," said Jessi, grinning.

"All in favour say 'aye'," Kristy added. When we all shouted "aye" she announced, "The 'ayes' have it!"

After that the phone got busy and we spent the rest of the meeting booking appointments and talking about nothing in particular. When the meeting broke up, Stacey, who was staying for dinner and then to tutor me, watched me put the note away in my jewellery box.

"Evidence," I explained.

"Right," said Stacey.

No matter how much junk food I eat, I'm usually hungry, but that night at dinner, I wasn't as hungry as I thought I would be. Could the thought of the tutoring session ahead possibly be affecting my appetite? I ate some more mashed potatoes and thought it over. No, not possible. After all, it was a tutoring session with my best friend.

Still, I didn't want seconds. When dinner was over, Janine started clearing the table (it was her turn).

"We can't study in the kitchen," I said quickly, in case Stacey had any ideas.

"Janine's going to be putting stuff away and clearing up after dinner."

"No problem," said Stacey. "I had a chance to talk to Janine and she suggested we use her room. It'll be less distracting than yours."

"Janine, you're a rat," I muttered, but not loudly enough for Stacey to hear, as I followed her to my room to get my books and then to Janine's room.

Talk about no distractions! My room is the original creative mess: paintings and posters on the wall, art supplies everywhere, hats and jewellery I've made hanging on an old brass hat stand in the corner, lots of colour—and I *do* know where (almost) everything is, in spite of how it looks.

Janine's room is precise. Perfectly organized. She keeps her shoes in a row in the wardrobe, and her clothes arranged according to colour and item. She cleans her room every Saturday morning. I don't bother with those things.

Now, sitting on the floor with Stacey, my back against the foot of Janine's bed, I started getting distracted by all that clean, empty space. If it were art, would it be called the absence of form? Or have something to do with negative space?

"Claudia," said Stacey warningly.

"Okay. Let's get started," I said. Resolutely, I picked up my English notebook.

"Look," I said, pulling the flash cards out of the back pocket of the notebook.

"Nice," said Stacey. "But did you learn the words?"

I was a little disappointed by Stacey's unenthusiastic response to my beautiful flash cards, but I reminded myself that it wasn't important here.

"Yes," I said. "Do you want to go over them?"

"Of course," replied Stacey. "Then we'll add new ones."

So we worked through the flash cards and I got all but one right. "Good," said Stacey when we'd finished. (She still didn't say anything about how great the flash cards looked.) "Work on 'peculiar' though, okay?" (That was the word I'd got wrong.)

"Okay," I replied crossly.

Stacey, who's usually quick to pick up on my moods, didn't register this at all. She was too busy turning into Mrs Hall.

We worked on sentence construction. We worked on changing words to nouns, adverbs and verbs. We worked on about a thousand vocabulary words and I made some new flash cards.

"Want to decorate these now?" I asked hopefully as I finished copying the last one.

"We could go to my room and work on them."

With a frown, Stacey shook her head. "This is serious, Claud. Don't forget it. Look, here, I've got something for you."

My feelings, which had been turning, well, negative, abruptly grew warm and positive again. Stacey had got me a surprise, to cheer me up and cheer me on.

Stacey handed me a black and white marbled notebook.

At first I was puzzled. Then I realized it was probably for sketching in. I used them sometimes in school. (Okay, I admit I use them during non-art classes, because they don't look so much like official sketch-books). It was nice of Stacey to try and cheer me up, I thought, feeling guilty about my cranky thoughts. "Thanks, Stace. What a nice surprise. I'm sure I'll be able to use this."

"I know you will," said Stacey, sounding more school-teachery than ever.

Uh-oh! I thought.

"It's for your journal."

"My journal? I don't keep a journal."

"You do now. Look, Claudia, it's the best way to practise all this stuff we've been revising. You use it in actual sentences and paragraphs, real writing—either by writing stories or by keeping a diary."

"Oh," I said weakly.

"So you're going to keep a journal. You can write anything you want in it. Then I'll read it and correct your spelling, punctuation, and so on."

"Gosh, thanks," I said. And if I sounded sarcastic, it was because I meant to.

Again, Stacey didn't even seem to notice. "Well," she said. "That about covers it."

In a daze I helped Stacey gather everything up and carry it back to my room.

"Why don't you get started on that journal?" suggested Stacey. "You don't need to walk me to the door."

"Fine," I said.

"We'll have another session this weekend. See you then."

"Not if I see you first," I muttered as Stacey left.

Keep a journal! Stacey correcting my private thoughts and words! Telling me what to do! Totally humourless and a pain—that's what Anastasia McGill was becoming.

I'd keep a journal all right. I'd give Stacey a real eyeful. Only it would be a secret journal.

I pulled out an old sketch book, only this one didn't have lined paper. It was only partly used. I flipped past the sketches, wrote the date and time at the top of the first piece of blank paper, and began my secret journal.

Anastasia McGill is a pill. I am glad shes helping me studey. I know I need all the help I can get, espesially sinse I don't want to fail english. But I don't like being bossed around like I am some two year old child. But the morre Stacy treats me like child, the moore I want to act like a child. That's not as bad as how Stacey is acting, tho. She should see herself. Hah.

And underneath that I drew a caricature of Stacey as a pointed-nosed schoolteacher holding a ruler. After that it was easy to open the real journal and write:

Today I babysat for the Rodowsky's. Shay is unhappy. I tried to help him with his homework, but he didnt like it.
It is peculiar to have Stacey tutoring me. But it would be very embarrasing to fail english. I will be glad when this test is over.

And you know what, I looked up *every single* word (except Rodowsky and Shea and Stacey). I wasn't going to let Stacey catch me making a single mistake if I could help it.

8th CHAPTER

Saturday

We had a Krushers' practice today and it was a killer. (Maybe we should call ourselves Kristy's Killers. Just kidding.) Anyway, about everything that could go wrong, did. Nothing major, a sort of chain reaction. And on top of that, after I'd scheduled the practice, Mrs. Korman asked me to sit for her, so that meant that not only were Bill and Melody there at practice as usual, but Skylar came also, so I was a coach _and_ a baby sitter. I wonder if major league coaches feel this way?

Kristy's Krushers are always ready to play ball, and that morning was no exception. Everyone turned out, plus, of course, Skylar. At one and a half, Skylar's a little too young to play ball, even with the Krushers, but she's not too little to enjoy being outside with everybody and wandering into the middle of things if she isn't watched closely.

It was an unusually hot day. Most of the Krushers had shed their sweatshirts almost immediately and Kristy, who's always prepared, had made them smear sunscreen on their noses and arms. She put sunscreen on Skylar, too, who didn't like it much. "No! No! Go! Go!" she kept saying.

"Okay," said Kristy, holding Skylar's hand as she addressed the Krushers. Skylar, who isn't always steady on her feet, kept swaying back and forth and pulling Kristy off balance. Kristy had to keep leaning back and forth as she talked.

"Okay," she said again. "We're going to practise throwing the ball to each other and catching people out. I'm going to put some of you in positions around the field and the rest of you are going to run the bases and get caught out."

Claire Pike, who's prone to throwing tantrums, pushed her lower lip out and said, "Not fair. I don't want to be caught out."

"You might not be," said Kristy. "We're practising. We're practising trying to catch the runner out and the runner is practising trying not to get caught out. And we'll all take turns."

It took a little while to organize everybody. Kristy, in a very cowardly way, put Claire in right field first instead of letting her be a runner. She kept Claire in close (since Claire's only five and can't throw the ball far), and put James Hobart behind her for backup. But once everyone was in position, she thought practice was going to go smoothly.

"Good, good!" she shouted as Buddy Barrett caught a grounder and threw it to third base, forcing Matt Braddock to retreat to the safety of second base. "That's called cutting off the runner. With no runner on first, and no chance of getting the runner to first out, that's exactly what you do. And good base-running, Matt!" She held up her hands and signed "good" so Matt could see her. Matt, who's deaf, waved and then turned to his sister Haley, who was watching from the sidelines. Her hands flew as she translated what Kristy had just said.

"Okay, let's try that a few more times . . ."

Kristy dipped to the left as Skylar tugged on her hand. "Wah!" said Skylar.

"Thirsty, Skylar? Okay, let's go and get a drink of water." She and Skylar walked to the water fountain by the dugout and Kristy lifted Skylar up for a drink, thinking how funny it was that Skylar would want to drink out of the park fountain when she was so afraid of the big fountain in the entry hall of her own house (well, mansion, really), that the Kormans couldn't even turn it on. But before Kristy could press the button to turn the water on, Skylar beat her to it. She pressed the button *hard*.

Water shot out of the fountain, splashing them both.

"Waaaaah!" screamed Skylar, twisting away so hard that Kristy stumbled backwards, crashed into a fence, and slid to the ground.

"Ooof!" said Kristy. The fall had knocked the wind out of her.

But not out of Skylar. She took a deep breath and screamed even louder.

"It's . . . okay . . . Skylar . . . see?" Kristy gasped, getting her breath back. "Just . . . a little water . . ."

"Noooo!" screamed Skylar.

Play on the field stopped. Everyone turned to see what was causing the screaming.

"Play . . . ON!" shouted Kristy. (Her breath had come back.)

Obediently the Krushers kept playing. But it took Kristy a long time to persuade Skylar to stop crying. And she had to walk the long way around the water fountain to get back to the field.

Kristy propped Skylar on her hip and surveyed the field.

"Time to put some new fielders and runners in," she announced, and switched everybody around.

"Let's try getting people out at first base," said Kristy. "This is the situation. No one on first, batter up. She hits the ball and runs to first. What do you do?"

"Catch the ball and catch her out!" said Jackie Rodowsky.

"Or if the ball was a fly ball she'd be out anyway," said Bill Korman.

"Or you can throw the ball to first base," said Linny Papadakis. "Or touch first base while you're holding the ball."

"Excellent. One hundred per cent right," said Kristy. "So let's do it. I'm going to hit the ball and Jackie's going to run to first base. Positions, everyone."

Kristy put Skylar in her buggy, fished around in the bag attached to the buggy, and came up with a banana.

"Here, Skylar. Want a banana?"

"Nana," said Skylar. Kristy peeled the banana and gave it to Skylar. Skylar waved the banana triumphantly back and forth. Then she squeezed it in her fist and began licking the banana that oozed out between her fingers. Messy, but effective, Kristy decided. She buckled Skylar into her buggy, wheeled the buggy into the dugout behind the fence, put on the brake, and went back to hit for the Krushers.

Kristy hit a gentle looping ball just to the left of first base.

Jackie began to run madly towards the plate.

The ball dipped down, down, down. It just missed the tip of Melody Korman's outstretched glove.

It landed on Jackie's head.

"Oh, no!" cried Kristy. Still holding the bat, she hurried towards Jackie.

Jackie didn't even slow down. He jumped on first base with both feet and said, "I made it, I made it!"

That was when Kristy realized he hadn't even felt the ball through his batting helmet.

"Are you okay, Jackie?" she asked.

He looked puzzled. "I'm fine."

"You're out," said Linny.

"No, I'm not," said Jackie.

"You are," said Linny.

"Why?"

"Linny's right," said Kristy. "If the ball

81

touches you while you're running the bases, you're out."

"Then why don't we just throw the ball at people?" asked Melody.

"Because it has to be an accident," said Kristy desperately. "Jackie, are you sure you're okay?"

"The ball didn't touch me!" Jackie was indignant.

Kristy hid a smile. "I'm afraid it did, Jackie. It landed on your batting helmet."

Jackie thought it over, then said, "Oh." He grinned. "Can we try again?"

"Of course. Practice makes perfect. Places everyone!" Kristy headed back to home plate.

Just then a horrible shriek came from Skylar. "TAT! TAT!"

Kristy had been keeping an eye on Skylar, of course, and she knew there was no cat around. (Skylar's terrified of cats.) She trotted towards Skylar, saying as soothingly as she could, "There aren't any cats, Skylar." She laid the bat down next to the buggy. "It's okay."

"TAT!" shrieked Skylar, deafening Kristy in one ear.

She pointed and Kristy straightened up and turned to see a woman standing near the third base line holding a small black dog.

"That's a dog," said Kristy.

"Tat!" insisted Skylar, but she sounded a little less certain.

The woman, who was standing close enough to Kristy and Skylar to hear the conversation, looked amused.

"He really is a dog," she called. "A schipperke. His name is Skipper." She leaned and put the dog down. He was wearing a red collar with a matching lead. Seeing his bright black button eyes, Kristy thought he looked more like a fox than a cat.

The dog grinned a dog grin and bounced happily up on his hind legs, watching the baseball being thrown back and forth on the field. "Arrf! Arrf, arrf, arrf!" he barked.

"See, Skylar, his name's Skipper and he's a dog," said Kristy.

Skylar looked wary but less frightened. "Tat?" she asked softly.

"Arf!" said Skipper.

"Dog," said Kristy.

"Dok," said Skylar.

"Yes," Kristy agreed, relieved.

Skylar leaned forward and stared, suddenly fascinated.

"Are you okay, now, Skylar?" asked Kristy. "Do you want to get out of your buggy and come with me?"

Skylar ignored her. So Kristy returned to what was left of practice. It didn't last much longer, and the rest of it went pretty smoothly.

After practice, Kristy walked the Kormans home (they live across the street from Kristy), pushing Skylar's buggy and listening to Bill and Melody talk. Skylar was asleep, worn out by the attack of the water fountain and the sneakiness of a dog disguised as a cat.

Practice had made Kristy think about Bart's Bashers, and in particular about Bart. Kristy will tell you that she's not ready for boys and all that stuff, but she does like Bart, who's the coach of the Krushers' rival team.

From thinking about Bart it was only a short jump to thinking about the notes that had arrived at the Babysitters Club meetings that week. The more Kristy thought about it, the more certain she was that Bart had sent the notes to her. "The best", for example. That sounded like something Bart would say. It was high praise from the coach of a softball team, and just the sort of phrase a coach would use. And besides, that's how Kristy and Bart's more-than-just-friendship had started in the first place—with anonymous notes Bart had sent Kristy.

Bart *had* to be the note-sender, Kristy concluded. It was his way of leading up to an invitation to the Spring Dance.

Mrs Korman returned a short time after Kristy, Bill, Melody and Skylar got home. But Kristy had had enough time to think up a plan. So the moment she left the Kormans' she hurried across the street to her house and got dressed up.

Not in a dress, of course. But she put on a denim skirt and her favourite polo-neck, tights to match, and slip-on shoes. She even pulled her hair back in a hairband.

Checking herself in the hall mirror, she made a face. "Oh, lord!" she breathed. Still, it was worth it for Bart. After all, look at the trouble he was going to with those notes.

When Kristy reached Bart's house, he was shooting baskets at the hoop attached to the side of the garage.

"Kristy, hey!" Bart waved to her to join him. She stood by him as he looped a shot towards the basket. It bounced once on the rim and went in.

"You're the best," said Kristy, giving Bart a Significant Look.

Bart grinned. "I wouldn't say that. Here, do you want to play? How about twenty-one?"

"You're nice," Kristy tried again.

Bart looked puzzled. "Okay," he said. "Do you want to go first?"

Then he noticed what Kristy was wearing. "Hey! Are you going somewhere special? Why are you all dressed up?"

Kristy felt her face going red. "I just felt like it, I suppose."

"Can you play dressed like that?" asked Bart. Then he added hastily, "I mean, it looks nice and everything, but . . ."

"I can play," said Kristy quickly. She picked up the ball and began to dribble it.

After the game, which Kristy almost won, Bart said, "I suppose you *can* play basketball dressed like that. Want to play another game?"

"Thanks, but I have to get home for lunch. See ya!"

"Okay," said Bart. "Good game."

"You too," replied Kristy.

She hurried home and changed into her usual clothes before joining her family for lunch. She was embarrassed by what had happened, even if Bart hadn't seemed to notice much. Also, she was no closer to finding out who was sending the BSC notes.

9th
CHAPTER

Time can go pretty quickly even if you're not having fun. It was Monday afternoon again (already), one week since I'd got the bad news about English, one week closer to the English test, and less than a week since my best friend had turned into the tutor monster.

And despite the tutoring, I still had the uneasy feeling I was going to fail the test.

I tried to think things through calmly. Claudia, I told myself, take a deep breath and imagine the worst thing that could happen. Fear of the unknown and the imagined is worse than fear of the known, right? (I mean, look at all those horror films about *something* lurking in the lake, woods, camp, or haunted house.)

So I took a deep breath and visualized: me sitting in the resource room, surrounded by people who hated being there as much as I did and who, no doubt just like me, would also be on all kinds of probation, like no babysitting club until their grades improved, no going out with their friends, no going to the shopping mall, no art, no leaving their rooms, allowed to eat only bread and water and possibly green vegetables . . .

Okay, so I was exaggerating a little bit. Unfortunately, visualizing the worst didn't make me feel any better.

Then I remembered my journals. Maybe writing some of my fears down would help. If I could put them on paper, maybe I could put them out of my mind. Sometimes that worked for a drawing or a painting. Only you know what? I'm never quite satisfied. I always finish a piece and think, I can do better than that. I know I can. I suppose that's why I keep trying.

I pulled out my journals and flipped open the official one. Each entry was neatly dated. And pretty short. I mean, how much can you write about the weather, what you ate for lunch at school, what you gossiped about at the BSC meetings, what you wore to school, and that kind of thing? Yawn. Big double yawn. But no way was I going to write real stuff down and let Stacey read it and act like the Evil Alien Teacher and put red marks and corrections all over it.

Besides, looking up practically every single word in the dictionary was a real pain.

I made a quick entry in the Official Journal:

Today at school we had gray meatloaf, some very orange carrots, yellow mashed potatoes, and lime green jellow. It did not taste very good. Cokey was wearing a lime green dress that matched the jellow. The color was better on the jellow.

We have a Baby-siters meeting today.

Good. That was done with. I sneaked a look at the clock. I had time before the meeting to write in my other journal, too.

I left the official journal on my desk with all my other books and pulled the other one out from the bottom of my desk drawer.

I wrote the date and time at the top, thought for a second, and then started writing.

I'm in my room. Its almost time for the meeting. Mondays are crummey. Today espeshally. Becuase Stacey (my possibly soon to be X best freind) has turned into the tuder monster. No kidding. She carests everything I do, like she's my pairents or something.

And I don't even think its helping. I feel as dumb as ever. Dummer. Im never going to be able to learn enough to pass the test. Never, ever, ever. I'll be in the Resorses Room for the rest of my life.

Well, at least when I fail the test, Stacey will stop beeing awfull.

Ugh oh. Its time to go. I just herd someone at the front door.

Hastily I closed my diary and stuck it in the drawer. Then I checked the clock. Wow! Whoever it was had arrived really early.

The door opened and my heart sank. It was Stacey. She smiled and held up her English book. "I knew you weren't sitting today, and I didn't have a job either, so I decided to come over early for a little extra tutoring."

"You didn't have to do that," I managed to say. But I was thinking, how pushy. She could at least have asked me if I wanted to study.

"No problem," said Stacey. "Come on, get your stuff and let's go to the kitchen."

"But the meeting! I mean, have we got enough time?"

"Plenty of time if you hurry up. Get everything together and I'll meet you

90

downstairs." Stacey looked at her watch. "You've got three minutes."

Well, I didn't need three minutes. I slammed everything together as loudly as I could before Stacey was halfway down the hall. And I dropped all my stuff pretty loudly on the kitchen table when I got there.

"Come on, Claudia," said Stacey impatiently. "Get it together. Let me see your journal."

I handed her the journal and plopped down in the chair opposite her. Stacey flipped it open, picked up a pencil (and it *was* red) and began to read.

I felt a smug expression forming on my face. Let her find any mistakes! Nearly every word was dictionary approved.

"Hmm," said Stacey. She read quickly through the journal, flipped back to the beginning—and began to write all over it in red!

I watched in disbelief. Then I said, "Hey!"

"Hmm?" said Stacey again, busily red-lining away.

"What are you doing?"

"Correcting your mistakes, Claud, what do you think?"

"Like what?"

"Well, like 'it's'."

"What about it? I mean, 'its'?" I couldn't believe my eyes.

"Look," said Stacey. She held the journal so I could see it. "It's got an apostrophe in it."

"That's only for the possessive," I said triumphantly. "Like if you said, 'Claudia's journal.' Look, I'll show you."

But before I could find the section in my English book, Stacey shook her head in a really maddening, smugly superior way. "Nope. That rule doesn't apply to the possessive of 'its'. You only use an apostrophe when you want to shorten 'it is'. Think of the apostrophe as replacing the 'i' in 'is'."

"That's the daftest thing I've ever heard! It's inconsistent. How am I supposed to learn to spell anything if they keep changing the rules?"

"It's not a hard rule to remember," said Stacey impatiently. She bent her head over my journal and her hand flew across the pages, making notes and circles and x's.

When she had finished, my perfect journal looked like the victim of a notebook murder.

I was steaming. And thinking about a little tutor murder, frankly.

It was a good thing the front door slammed when it did.

I looked at my watch (surprisingly enough, Stacey hadn't made me take it off to stop it distracting me) and said, "Five twenty-nine. That must be Kristy."

"Okay. We can stop," said Stacey.

"Thanks!" I muttered sarcastically.

Soon everybody was assembled in my room, the phone was ringing, Mary Anne was scheduling appointments for all of us (except me) and I was drowning my troubles in a chocolate Snickers bar.

At 5.45 Dawn checked her watch. Then she looked at me. "Where's Janine?"

I shook my head. "Don't know. She's got a meeting at school or something. I think."

"Well, I'm going to check your front door." Dawn stood up and dashed downstairs. A minute later she returned, a white envelope held triumphantly aloft in her hand.

"Another note!" said Kristy.

"Oooh!" said Mary Anne, clasping her hands together.

"Just like the others," announced Dawn. "Same envelope and" (she opened the envelope and unfolded the piece of paper) "same kind of paper."

"What does it say?" asked Mallory.

"'You are the greatest'," read Dawn.

"I knew it!" said Stacey.

"Knew what?" I snapped. It was the first

93

time during the meeting that I'd spoken to her.

"That it's from Sam, of course. I'm positive it's from Sam."

"You really think so?" asked Jessi. "Why?"

Before Stacey could answer, I exploded. "For you? From Sam? Give me a break! Who's died and left you the only person on earth who could get a note from someone?"

"What?" said Stacey.

"Oh, that's right. You are the greatest. It's—let me spell that for you, such a simple rule, really, I-t-, apostrophe for the letter i, s—it's obvious to all of us that you are the greatest one here. So it must be for you."

By the time I'd finished, Stacey's face was the colour of her correcting pencil. And she exploded right back at me: "Well, excuse me, Claudia Kishi! Excuse me for trying to help you! Excuse me for expecting you to want to work on passing English. Excuse me for being your friend!"

"You're excused," I replied. "So why don't you just go!" I got up and marched to the door of my room and flung it open.

Stacey didn't say another word. She just grabbed her rucksack and stormed out.

Everyone else sat there like life-sized soft sculptures, in various poses that could be labelled everything from "shock" (Mary Anne) to "amazement" (Kristy).

The phone rang. Kristy looked at it, frowned at it, then picked it up. "Babysitters Club," she said.

I stared stonily out of my window as Kristy and Mary Anne arranged one more job for the day.

Then I looked at my watch. Very pointedly.

Kristy checked hers. "Six o'clock. This meeting is officially adjourned."

Murmuring polite goodbyes, everybody walked quietly out of the door.

"Goodbye," I said as the door shut behind Mallory, who was the last to leave.

I reached in my drawer, pulled out my secret journal, picked up my pen, and really let Stacey have it.

10th CHAPTER

It was raining. Which about matched my mood. But a good babysitter doesn't take her moods to work, so I tried to put mine to one side and concentrate on the Rodowskys.

Actually, I didn't really have to concentrate on Jackie and Archie. They'd hung around for a little while, making suggestions about snacks and snacktime, while trying to decide if it was ever going to stop raining so they could go outside.

After asking me for the tenth time if I thought the rain would stop (and after my answering that I didn't know when, but I hoped *soon*), Jackie grabbed Archie by the sleeve and dragged him off to the playroom. So all I had to do was listen for any ominous crashes.

Shea, who looked like I felt as he sat in an armchair by the window, his elbow on one arm of the chair and his chin in his hand, staring out at the rain, finally heaved an enormous sigh. "Well, I'd better go and start my homework," he said. "It'll probably take about ten hours, since I'm so stupid."

I *almost* said cheerfully, "Oh, Shea, you're not stupid. You just . . ." etc, etc, etc. But I didn't. Possibly my bad mood acted like some kind of truth drug.

Anyway, instead of joining the chorus of people telling Shea how bright he was (despite what must have seemed like proof to the contrary), I sighed myself. Deeply.

"I know what you mean," I said. "*Not* that you're stupid. I don't believe that's true. And I don't believe I'm stupid, either. But it takes me *hours* to do my homework, too. Unless I just decide to skip it."

"I wish I could skip it," Shea answered. "But people keep checking up on me." He glanced at me, looking a little suspicious, and a little puzzled. "Anyway, it *should* take you hours to do your homework. You're in eighth grade. I'm only in fourth."

"Not true," I answered. "No matter what grade you're in, it's not supposed to take you mega-hours to do your homework. At least, I don't think it is." I paused for a minute, then said, "You know, Shea, I should have told you this before, the last time I was here with you boys . . . I'm having a terrible time in school. If I don't pass my next English test, I might even fail English. And that means I'll have to go to the resource room. Back to it, I mean. I've been there before."

Shea turned away from the window and stared at me. "Really?"

"Yup. People are always telling me I'm clever and I should do well in school and I should try harder. But it just doesn't work that way. I'm good at some things, but school isn't one of them. Ask me about other things, such as art. I'm *excellent* at those subjects."

"Me, too. I mean, I'm a pretty good athlete."

"Good? You're great. I've seen you playing ball with Jackie and Archie."

Shea thought about that for a minute. Then he smiled a little. "Yeah, I am pretty good," he said.

"I wish I could do my English homework like you play baseball," I told him. "Then this test would be a cinch. And I wouldn't have to spend all my free time being tutored for it, either."

"You've got a tutor?" Shea's voice rose in surprise. He looked around, but Jackie and Archie were nowhere to be seen. Shea lowered his voice. "I hate having a tutor.

The one I have at school is so *cheerful*. He always says 'good' even when my work isn't."

"My tutor," I said, "never says 'good'. She just bosses me around. It's a real pain. She's even making me keep a journal and she corrects all the mistakes and spelling in it."

"Do you have trouble spelling?"

"You'd better believe it!" I said fervently.

"Me, too! Hey, Claudia?"

"Hey, Shea, what?"

"Would you—could you help me with my homework today? Not all of it, but maybe my spelling?"

I couldn't believe it. Someone was asking me, Claudia Lynn Kishi, for help with spelling. But I stayed calm. Outwardly. "Okay. I could do that. But," I added as Shea and I went to find his books, "only if I can see the words. Otherwise, I probably won't know how to spell them."

And Shea actually laughed.

We got Shea's spelling lists and settled down in the living room. "How do you want to do this?" I asked.

"You say the word and I'll write it down. Then we check to see if I've spelled it right."

Shea handed me the list. Slowly we

worked our way down. I have to confess, I was surprised. First, I thought the words were pretty hard, especially for a fourth-grader. Secondly, I could spell a lot of them anyway—I even remembered some of them from looking them up nineteen million times for my official journal. Thirdly, Shea was good. Very slow, though. He'd learned some new rules for spelling, and often he would just write a letter down and stare at it, before putting it into a word, but he got a lot of those words right.

"Peace," I said, reaching the last word. "Like in 'peace and quiet'."

"P" wrote Shea, only he wrote it back to front. I almost said something. But I didn't. "P points towards the end," Shea muttered. He rubbed out the letter and wrote it facing the other way. Then he wrote the rest of the word very carefully, very slowly.

And exactly right.

"Shea, that's great!" I cried. Then I paused, a little embarrassed. "Um, how did you know it was spelled 'e-a-c-e'?"

Shea understood what I meant. "You mean the 'e' coming before the 'a'?"

"Uh-huh. Is that a rule, too?"

"Nope." Shea grinned mischievously. "But you know what? It almost always does, so I just always put it down that way. I'm *usually* right."

100

I was really impressed that he'd taken the time to work that out. And that he'd been able to.

"What about 'piece' like in 'a piece of cake'?"

Shea quoted, " 'I' before 'e' except after 'c'. Only I'm never sure if an 'i' is even supposed to be in the word. It would make more sense to spell it p-e-c-e."

"True. Listen," I said impulsively, "would you help me with *my* spelling?"

"You mean *I* get to be the teacher?"

"Yes." I handed Shea a magazine. "Pick some words out and help me learn to spell them."

Shea looked at the magazine I'd chosen. *Seventeen*. "How about *Sports Illustrated* instead?" he suggested.

"You can choose your magazines, I choose mine," I declared.

"Oh, all right," said Shea, grinning. He opened the magazine. "Peach," he said.

"Peach?" I repeated.

"It's the colour of a nail varnish," explained Shea.

"Oh," I said. "P . . ." I looked at Shea. I thought about using two 'e's. I remembered Shea's rule. "E-a."

I stopped. Shea nodded.

"T-c-h," I muttered. No. That didn't sound right.

101

"Think of other words that sound like it," suggested Shea.

"Reach," I said. "Teach."

"Beach," said Shea.

"Beach? I know how to spell beach," I said.

"Peach?" asked Shea.

"The same!" I said triumphantly. "P-e-a-c-h."

"Yes!" Shea dropped the magazine and pumped both fists in the air as if I'd just hit a home run.

After that I hardly noticed the rain, or the relative p-e-a-c-e at Jackie and Archie's end of the house. And by the time they'd returned to the family room to make some more snack suggestions (it really was snacktime by now), I'd started feeling a little better about my creative spelling abilities. Shea had been a *huge* help.

When Mrs Rodowsky came home, Shea had finished his homework. We met her in the front hall, like before, but the vibes between Shea and me were a lot better.

In fact, they were great.

Shea followed me out on to the front porch. "Thanks," he said.

"Hey, Shea? Thank *you*."

I put up my umbrella and walked home, almost singing in the rain.

Wait till I told Stacey!

Then I remembered. Stacey and I weren't speaking. Since our fight we'd had one tutoring session, a session of extreme politeness, and we'd been cordial in the BSC meetings.

But that was all.

I couldn't just go home, call Stacey, and tell her about Shea. Unless I apologized.

I wasn't ready to do that. I was still pretty angry with Stacey about her killer teacher attitude. She'd been so caught up in trying to act like a teacher that she'd forgotten to act like a friend. I'd become some kind of project for Stacey. And that didn't help. No way.

When I reached home, I dug out my secret journal and wrote:

Today Shay asked _me_ to tooter him! I helped him with his spelling. He is one smart kid. Becuase of his learning disabilaty, its hard, maybe imposible for him to learn to spell words the reguler way. So hes figyured out all these rules and things to help him remerber.

And they work! I know becuase Shay helped me with my spelling too

He was a _exsellent_ tutor. Even though it was just him and me, he didnt make me fell like the class dummy

He did what a real, good tuter is suposed to do - he helped me learn.

Unlike some bossy tuters who are suposed to be your freind but never say any thing nice about your work, Shay said nice things. And he meant them. Unlike some mean tuters, Shay was nice. A peach.

No. I wasn't ready to apologize to Stacey. I wasn't ready to make peace.

11th CHAPTER

Saturday

Whoa. Friday night at Kristy's house was some hard work (but then, unlike some people, I don't mind working hard). David Michael was in a, well, creative mood. Only his creativity sort of backfired on him, I guess. Of course, when children goof around, they seem funny, instead of childish and irresponsible. So even if the night was hard work, it was fun hard work ...

When Stacey reached Kristy's house on Friday night, the phrase "the lights were on but no one was at home" came to mind. I mean, it's a big house, but everyone except Nannie, David Michael and Emily Michelle had left: Kristy to Bart's school to watch him play in a basketball game, Charlie on a date, Sam with his friends to the cinema and Kristy's mum and step-father to a film at the college (that's different from going to the cinema, you know). Karen and Andrew Brewer were at their mum's that weekend, and Nannie, who met Stacey at the door, was on her way to a dinner party.

"Wow, you look *nice*!" exclaimed Stacey when Nannie opened the front door. Then she was embarrassed. "Not that you don't always. I mean, you know . . ."

Nannie's eyes twinkled. "I know. You don't often see me in anything but trousers."

Grateful that Nannie understood, Stacey nodded. "That's a terrific dress. Pink really is your colour."

Nannie was wearing a pink silk dress with a wide twisted silver and pink sash, sparkly silvery earrings and these really cool flat pale silver shoes.

Stacey wasn't the only one impressed by Nannie's appearance. David Michael and

Emily Michelle were staring at Nannie as she checked her hair one last time in the hall mirror. Giving it a quick pat, Nannie picked up her bag and cape and said, "You know where everything is, of course, Stacey. David Michael had seconds of dessert tonight, so he can have a glass of milk before bed, and some fruit if he wants it, but no more sweets . . ."

"Aww," said David Michael.

"The same for Emily Michelle, although she usually doesn't want anything once she starts getting sleepy . . . Mr and Mrs Brewer will be back around eleven. The numbers where we can be reached are on the notice board above the phone in the kitchen. And that's it."

"Have a good time," said Stacey.

"Thank you," Nannie replied. She waved at everyone and then slipped out of the door.

Stacey turned to look at the two kids.

"Hello," she said.

"Hi," said David Michael.

Emily Michelle stared solemnly.

"Not talking? That's cool. What do you want to do?"

David Michael made an elaborate show of looking over each shoulder. Then he said in a loud whisper, "Play haunted house."

That caught Stacey off guard. If he had

been Karen Brewer, she would have been expecting it, since Karen has a very vivid imagination and exercises it regularly, by doing things like convincing herself that the old woman next door is really a witch named Morbidda Destiny. But David Michael's usually a little more realistic.

"Haunted house?" repeated Stacey. Even as she said the words, she knew it probably wasn't a good idea. It sounded like just the sort of game that would scare kids into staying awake and over-excited, long past their bedtime. "Um, David Michael . . ."

"We turn off all the lights, and we get a torch and we go from room to room looking for ghosts!"

"It sounds fun. And scary," Stacey said. "But I don't think it's a good idea to play that tonight."

"Why not?" asked David Michael.

"It'd probably be *too* scary."

"Not for me."

"But maybe for Emily. And," Stacey added, pretty truthfully, "definitely for me!"

"Can we read ghost stories, then? I've got a new collection of scary, *true* ones." David Michael started back towards the family room and Stacey and Emily trailed after him.

Stacey asked, "What's all this ghost stuff? It's not even Hallowe'en."

But she sat down on the sofa in the family room, pulled Emily up next to her and took the book David Michael handed her. "I know this one," said Stacey. "Dawn's got *Scary Stories to Tell in the Dark* in her scary story collection. There are two more of these, too."

"Oh, boy!" said David Michael. He sat down next to Stacey.

She flipped through the pages until she found a story that was more funny than scary, and started reading. When she had finished, David Michael said, "That was good. Can we read another?"

But Stacey had decided that one story was enough, especially with Emily Michelle sitting attentively next to her. Who knew what Emily was making of it all?

"Not right now," said Stacey.

To her surprise, David Michael didn't argue. He jumped off the sofa and said, "Then may I be excused for a minute?"

"Okay," replied Stacey. David Michael left and Stacey said to Emily, "So, Emily, what's happening?"

"Emily," said Emily. Her face split into an unexpected smile.

Stacey smiled back. "Most definitely, Emily. You are most definitely what's happening." She turned one of Emily's hands up and softly slapped her five.

Emily's grin turned into giggles. So Stacey gave Emily five on her other hand and then on the soles of her feet, which made Emily giggle even harder. They were still giggling a few minutes later when Stacey realized that David Michael hadn't come back.

"David Michael!" called Stacey.

No answer.

"David Michael?" she called, louder this time.

Still no answer.

"Uh-oh, Emily. Come on." Stacey stood up, took Emily by the hand, and went off in search of David Michael. Just as they reached the hall, the lights in the house flickered—and went off.

"David Michael, stop that!" she called, suddenly realizing just how *big* the Brewer mansion was. And how empty. And how full of dark, dark rooms . . .

"S-Stacey?" David Michael's voice sounded a little quavery.

Trying to remain calm, Stacey bent over to pick Emily up, then took a deep breath. "David Michael, where are you? Turn those lights back on!" Stacey just *knew* that David Michael was trying to trick her into playing haunted house.

And she wasn't going to fall for it.

David Michael didn't answer. And it was in the little moment of silence that followed that Stacey realized how *really* dark it was. When she looked out of the window, she couldn't see any street lights or lights from other houses.

David Michael couldn't have done that, could he? No, of course not. It had to be some kind of power cut. And David Michael was somewhere in the house in the dark, probably a little scared.

"David Michael, the power has just gone off outside. It's nothing serious. Stay where you are while I get a torch. Okay?"

"Okay," said David Michael at last. He sounded calmer.

Shifting Emily, who was getting heavy, Stacey groped her way to the kitchen and found the torch in the utility room drawer. She switched it on, reassured by the light, but not happy by all the shadows it suddenly cast.

Stop it, Stacey, she told herself. You're the responsible one here. The one in charge. The babysitter.

Ugh! That sounded just like the title of a horror book.

Shaking off thoughts of scary stories and ghosts and horror books, Stacey followed the beam of the light back into the hall.

"David Michael?" she called. "Where are you?"

"In the basement," he called back.

"The basement?" *What*, Stacey wondered, was David Michael doing in the basement? "Okay. Hang on. I'm on my way."

She and Emily crept towards the basement. When they reached the basement door, which was partly open, Stacey put Emily down and took her hand. Together, they made their way down the basement stairs.

At the bottom of the stairs, Stacey flashed the light around the basement. It was a huge jumble of all kinds of things (with all kinds of shadows, she noted unhappily). "David Michael?"

"Over here," said his voice from a dark corner.

Carefully leading Emily, Stacey began to pick her way across the basement.

She walked round an old wardrobe.

Then she jumped and began to scream.

David Michael began to scream.

Emily Michelle began to cry.

And the lights came back on.

Stacey stopped screaming, loosened her grip on Emily (which was probably one of the reasons Emily had started to cry), and began to murmur little soothing things to her. Emily snuffled a few times, then stopped to stare with puzzled wet eyes at her brother.

Who was wearing a long white sheet.

"David Michael, *what* are you doing?" demanded Stacey.

The ghost began to thrash around inside the sheet. At last a sheepish, red-faced David Michael emerged before Stacey and Emily Michelle. "I just wanted to scare you a little. I was going to make moaning sounds when you came to look for me and then jump out and say boo."

"Not funny, David Michael."

"Then the lights went out!" David Michael sounded indignant now. "I wasn't scared but . . . I thought maybe, you know, Ben Brewer . . ."

Ben Brewer was an ancestor of the Brewers. Karen (who else?) is convinced his ghost still lives in the house.

"It wasn't Ben Brewer, it was the electricity board. There must have been a power failure or something."

"Oh," said David Michael.

"Come on," said Stacey. "Let's have some milk, and a non-scary story, and then I think it's time for bed."

David Michael didn't argue. In fact, he was very, very good for the rest of the night.

Later, after she'd put David Michael and Emily Michelle to bed, Stacey had to laugh at the timing. Poor David Michael! He must have been terrified when the lights went out while he was down in the basement.

And he'd really scared her.

In fact, she still felt a little jumpy. With both children in bed, she was aware once again of the huge, silent house. She picked up a magazine, put it down, flipped through the TV channels, then gave up and picked up the phone.

Mary Anne was at home. "You won't believe what's just happened!" Stacey told her, and then recounted how David Michael had been outghosted by the electricity board.

"Poor David Michael," said Mary Anne sympathetically.

"Mary Anne!" cried Stacey. Then she realized that Mary Anne was laughing.

"At least it wasn't the secret admirer," said Mary Anne.

"Please!" said Stacey. "I'm not opening the door tonight to check for notes. I've had enough thrills for one evening."

"Oh, guess what?" Mary Anne said.

"You've heard from the secret admirer?"

"No. But Logan's asked me to the dance."

Stacey was pleased for Mary Anne. "Excellent. Did he say anything about the notes?"

"No, not a word. Not a clue. But Bart's asked Kristy, too. Maybe he's said something to her. You could ask her when she gets back."

"Good idea," said Stacey. They talked for a little while longer, then hung up. A few minutes later the phone rang, and Stacey picked it up.

"I'm going to the dance," Mallory announced. "With Ben Hobart."

"All right!" said Stacey. She and Mallory talked about it for a few minutes, along with other topics, like what to wear to the dance.

Afterwards, Stacey sat for a while, thinking about the notes. So far, Mary Anne and Logan were going to the dance, as were Bart and Kristy, Ben and Mallory, Jessi and Curtis Shaller, (Jessi had been the first one asked), and she was going with Sam.

But not one single boy had mentioned any anonymous love (or like) notes. And not one single boy was even acting suspiciously or suspiciously romantic.

Frustrating, thought Stacey. Maybe something was wrong with their theory about a secret admirer. Or maybe the notes were from some boy they hadn't thought of yet.

Stacey got up and checked David Michael and Emily, who were both asleep. Stacey was relieved that Emily didn't seem to have been affected by the "ghost" scare in the basement. She smiled again, thinking of how they had all scared each other.

She could hardly wait to tell Sam. She hoped he'd come home from the cinema before she left.

Back downstairs, Stacey settled down with a book and a diet Coke. She turned the pages dreamily and thought about going to the dance with Sam. It would be romantic, but it would be fun, too. That was the nice thing about Sam. When he wasn't acting wild and crazy, he was a lot of fun.

She wondered if he was sending the notes. If he wasn't, who was? Stacey tried to think of someone at school, some cute but shy boy, who might have been lingering near one of them. Try as she could, though, she couldn't think of a single candidate.

So if it wasn't some shy boy, and it wasn't someone they knew, *who was it*?

A ghost, thought Stacey wryly. Maybe the secret admirer was a ghost.

12th CHAPTER

In spite of everything awful that was going on in my life, I was feeling pretty pleased and flattered as I rang the Rodowskys' front doorbell. Why? Because at a BSC meeting on Monday, Mrs Rodowsky had called and specifically asked for me, Claudia Kishi, to come for a tutoring session with Shea. It was hard not to give Stacey a smug look of triumph as I said, "Well, I wasn't going to accept any more babysitting jobs till after the test. But in this case, I think I should make an exception."

So there I was on Wednesday afternoon, looking forward to a tutoring session!

Mrs Rodowsky seemed in a pretty cheerful mood, too.

"Come in, Claudia," she said, holding the door wide open. "I won't say Shea has been looking forward to more tutoring, but

I will say he's shown more enthusiasm at the idea of your helping him than he's shown about anything for a while."

"I suppose we get on well," I said. "You know, we've got some things in common and all."

Very articulate, Claudia, I told myself. But Mrs Rodowsky didn't seem to notice. She nodded and said, "Well, Shea's in his room. You know where it is."

"Thank you," I said.

Shea was in his room. His pose was a variation on the "I'll-sit-near-my-work-and-maybe-it-will-rub-off-on-me" position. I recognized it because it is one of my favourites. It means you spread out everything you have to do, and then you doodle or draw or do something else, anything else, on the top of all your work.

Shea had arranged his books like an obstacle course, and was rolling marbles down them.

"I'm betting on the blue marble," I said.

The blue marble rolled down one book, slid down a paper funnel, missed the gap between the end of the paper and the next book, hit the top of the desk and fell on to the floor.

Shea looked up at me and grinned. "You lose."

"You win some, you lose some," I

answered. "Come on. Let's get this tutoring stuff started."

"Okay," said Shea. He scooped the marbles into the desk drawer. "I've got five maths problems. Then I'm supposed to make a graph of the answers."

"Maths," I said. "Yuck!"

"Yeah," said Shea.

Fortunately, the problems weren't too complicated. In fact, the hardest part for Shea (who, once he understood what the problem was, could actually work it out in his head right away) was reading the problem correctly and then writing it down correctly. Since getting the answers right is *my* weak point, we soon had a pretty good system going. Sort of like this:

Shea: "No, it can't be a hundred and twenty-six. You forgot to divide by two."

Me: "Right. Let's see, half of one hundred and twenty-six is twelve divided by two is . . ."

Shea: "Sixty-three."

Me: "How did you do that?"

Shea (making an it-was-no-big-deal gesture, but looking pleased): "I don't know."

Me: "Pretty good, Shea. So now you have to write it out . . ." Then, "Wait, Shea. It's a hundred and twenty-*six*."

Shea (staring at the paper): "One, two . . ." (muttering) "Nine is above six . . .

And nine looks forwards, 'P' looks backwards." (Then rubbing out the "9" he'd written and putting a "6" in its place.)

Me: "Decent!"

Shea: "Yeah."

The graph was kind of fun. I'd come straight from school and I had my art pencils with me. So instead of just a plain old HB pencil graph, we made the graph in super colours like magenta and mango yellow.

"Outstanding," I said.

"Decent," agreed Shea. "The colours make it easier to follow."

"Yeah, and it doesn't look so much like maths homework!"

Shea finished shading in a section of the graph and said, "One day, when I'm grown up and finished with school, I'm going to invent an alphabet that doesn't have so many *slippery* letters in it. Or numbers either."

"That's a good idea," I said. "Why don't you just leave the numbers out altogether? I'd vote for that."

He considered the possibility, then said, "Maybe. Only we might need them to count money."

"Money's always a problem," I agreed.

"Yeah," he said. "You know, some languages don't have as many letters, like

Hawaiian. It doesn't have any 'V's and stuff like that."

"Cool. Pretty clever of the Hawaiians. But what about Chinese? That language has about two thousand alphabet characters. Or maybe it's twenty thousand, I forget. But lots, anyway." (I knew this from some research I'd done for a calligraphy class.)

"No way!" Shea made a gagging noise and let his head drop to one side and we both laughed.

"Maybe I'm lucky after all," he said.

"Well, you've finished your maths, anyway. Want to help *me* now?"

I pulled out my new flash cards (even though I was still cross with Stacey, I was doing what she'd suggested, and I'd made flash cards for all my vocabulary words now).

"Wow!" said Shea when he saw my decorations. "I'm going to decorate *my* flash cards!"

"I'll help you," I promised. "But first, help me with my vocabulary."

So we went through the flash cards.

"Only four mistakes out of twenty-five," said Shea. "Good work."

"Thank you," I said. "I wonder what grade that would be in a real test. If you have twenty-five answers and each answer is worth . . ."

"Four," said Shea. "Twenty-five goes into a hundred four times. So four mistakes times four is sixteen. The answer is eighty-four. A B."

"Pretty good," I said, impressed with my B and how quickly Shea had figured it out.

"Uh-huh!" said Shea. "But do you know what? I think you can do even better, Claudia."

How many times have people told me that? You can do better, just apply yourself. Try harder. Pay attention.

Oh, most of them mean well. Most of them want me to do better, for whatever reason.

But this was the first time I really believed it. Because Shea understood what it meant to hear these things. And he wouldn't say them lightly.

"Thanks," I said.

I smiled at him. He smiled at me.

We were sitting there grinning away at each other when his mother tapped on the door to tell me the tutoring session was over.

I grinned all the way back to my house for the BSC meeting. Unfortunately, Stacey and I arrived at the front door at the same time.

"Claudia," said Stacey, inclining her head slightly.

"Stacey," I replied, raising one eyebrow

in a very sophisticated way. I opened the door. "After you."

"Thank you," said Stacey. She went in and up the stairs. At the door to my room she stopped and opened it. "After you," she said.

"Thank you," I said.

To my relief I saw that every club member except Mary Anne was there. As Stacey sat down and I looked for junk food (as far from Stacey as I could), Mary Anne hurried in.

Kristy pulled her visor down and intoned, "This meeting of the Babysitters Club will come to order."

At exactly 5.45 the doorbell rang.

Dawn leapt up, ran across the room and looked out of the window. "Rats!"

"What? What?" cried Kristy.

"I bet it was the secret message person," said Dawn. "Why didn't I think of it before? We could have set a trap. We could have . . ."

"I'll go to the door," I said, and raced downstairs, since neither Janine nor my parents were home.

Taped to the door was an envelope, just like all the other envelopes. I peeled it free and raced back upstairs.

"I knew it!" exclaimed Dawn as I entered the room, waving it in the air.

"And the winner is . . ." I tore the envelope open and unfolded the sheet of paper.

"What does it say?" asked Jessi.

"You lot read it," I said, puzzled. I passed the note around.

This is what it said:

To the babysitters,
Please come and meet us at the Rosebud Cafe. Come on Saturday afternoon. We are inviting you because we like you. You are very special and we want to treat you.

"I knew it," said Kristy. She sniffed the note, then handed it back to me.

"The note is for *all* of us," I said.

"Smell it," suggested Kristy. "There's perfume on it."

"*We* are inviting you?" said Dawn. "Who's we? Ugh! That's *strong* perfume."

"I knew it," Kristy repeated. "Don't you see? Or rather smell? It's Cokie and Grace. They're at it again. That's Cokie's perfume! Don't they ever give up? Why don't they at least find a new game to play?"

Jessi frowned. "What do you think they're up to?"

"They think," explained Kristy, "that *we'll* think this note is from a lot of adoring boys and we'll get all dressed up and go to the cafe and no one will meet us. Or Cokie and Grace will be there to make fun of us. Or something."

"What rats!" cried Mallory. "What are we going to do?"

Folding her arms, Kristy said, "Leave it to me. I'll think of something."

"Another of Kristy's great ideas," teased Mary Anne.

Kristy nodded grimly. "You'd better believe it," she said.

Business took off for the last five minutes of the meeting, and the phone rang almost constantly. Then it was six o'clock and Kristy adjourned us. As everyone was leaving, Stacey hung back.

What now? I wondered. Was Stacey the Killer Tutor actually going to apologize?

If she did, I'd forgive her. I'd be generous and polite and kind and . . .

"Claud, I've got to correct your journal. Why don't you give it to me to take home?"

Huh? I thought.

Just then, Mary Anne stuck her head back in the door. "Claud—"

If Stacey wasn't going to apologize, I didn't have to be polite, right?

"What is it, Mary Anne?" I said sweetly.

"Claudia," said Stacey sharply.

"The journal's in the drawer," I practically snarled. Then I turned sweetly towards Mary Anne.

"Here," said Mary Anne looking from me to Stacey and back. "I almost forgot. I borrowed this magazine last Friday and I wondered if . . ."

"Where?" asked Stacey, slamming one drawer and pulling open another.

"Will you excuse me for a moment, Mary Anne? I'm *so* sorry about the interruptions."

"Never mind," snapped Stacey. "I've found it." She slammed the drawer shut and brushed past us.

I breathed a sigh of relief. Inside, I was boiling mad at Stacey all over again. But I suppose it didn't show too much. Because apart from glancing quickly at Stacey's departing back, Mary Anne didn't say anything. She smiled, handed me the magazine, and left.

13th CHAPTER

On Saturday afternoon I stood in front of my wardrobe staring at my clothes. I don't usually mind looking in the wardrobe. But the usual wardrobe rules that make it interesting—avoid wearing the exact same outfit twice, be outrageous, and look cool *and* terrific—didn't exactly apply today.

Today, I was trying to get ready to meet our secret admirers, Cokie and Grace, at the Rosebud Cafe. I was also trying to follow Kristy's instructions to look as awful as I could.

Hmm. Maybe I could borrow something of Janine's? No. If she found out why I wanted to borrow her clothes, she might be insulted. And she was bound to ask why I wanted them.

I pulled out an old pair of tattered jeans, studied them for a moment, then ripped the bottoms of the legs off. When I pulled them on, the ragged edge of one leg hung below my knee. The other made an uneven line above my knee.

So far, so good.

I hunted around in my wardrobe and found a big old lime green shirt with a bleached spot (it had got mixed up with a load of white clothes that were being bleached) near the bottom at the front. I put that on.

Pretty ratty.

And wrinkly.

Better and better.

I found a pair of socks. Bright green socks. Then I dug a pair of turquoise trainers out of the back of my wardrobe. I'd stopped wearing them because I'd poked a hole through one of the toes. I put those on and studied the effect in the mirror. A major clash of colours.

But my superior fashion sense told me something was still missing.

I reached up and took the tie out of my hair and let it fall. I shook my head a little to mess it up.

Jewellery? No.

What about make-up? Well . . .

I remembered an orange-red lipstick that I'd bought once (I think I was unconscious at the time) and never worn. I dug around in my make-up drawer and pulled it out.

I put the lipstick on, then stuffed a whoopee cushion into my shoulder bag. Having practical joke items is one of the benefits of being a babysitter. Not only had I once babysat for Betsy Sobak, one of the world's worst practical jokers—until with the help of one of Betsy's practical jokes I broke my leg—but Mallory's brothers and sisters are big fans of practical joke items, such as rubber spiders and fake sick. (Although maybe *fake* sick wasn't necessary when dealing with Cokie and Grace.)

Stepping back, I took another look at myself in the mirror.

I was definitely a strong candidate for the Worst Dressed Award. I couldn't wait to see what the others in the BSC were wearing. I also could hardly wait to see what joke items they'd bring.

I checked the clock radio and realized I'd have to wait a little longer. It wasn't quite time to head for the cafe. That was all right. I'd have a few extra minutes to write in my secret journal.

I put my bag by the door, sat down at my desk, and opened the drawer. At first I thought the journal had disappeared. Then I realized it had slid to the back of the drawer. I pulled it out, flipped it open, picked up my pen . . .

And screamed, *"Oh, no!"* The pen slipped out of my fingers. I grabbed the journal with both hands and held it up, hoping maybe I was getting short-sighted and wasn't really seeing what I was seeing.

But I was.

The journal I was holding wasn't my secret journal. It was the official one. Which could only mean that Stacey had the other one. The one with all the nasty, hateful things I'd written in it about her.

Never mind that I wasn't speaking to Stacey. Stacey was never going to speak to me again.

Ever.

I spent a few minutes wondering and worrying. (Maybe she hadn't read it yet. Maybe she'd realize after the first few lines it wasn't the right journal and stop reading. Maybe I should move to Mars.)

I remembered a book I'd read, *Harriet the Spy*. The same thing had happened to Harriet, I told myself, and she'd survived.

Hadn't she?

The numbers on the clock rolled over and I realized I didn't have time to worry any more. I had to hurry if I wanted to arrive at the Rosebud Cafe on time.

A few minutes later, as I neared the front of the cafe, I skidded to a stop. Good grief!

Who were those tacky, horrible, fashion nightmares standing around outside?

"Claud!" gasped Mallory. "You look *awful*."

Mallory, Jessi, Stacey, Kristy, Mary Anne and Dawn all stared at me, and I gaped back at them. (Although I couldn't bring myself to look directly at Stacey.)

They looked as bad as I did, a cacophony (that was a particularly creatively decorated spelling flash card of mine) of crazy colours, random wrinkles and disgusting dirt.

Dawn began to laugh.

"Shh!" said Kristy. "Keep it down. We don't want to give it away." She reached in her pocket and pulled out a water pistol. "Ready with your weapons!" Waving her water gun, she pushed open the door to the cafe.

Dawn put her hand over her mouth, but she couldn't help snorting through her nose as we followed Kristy inside.

The cafe was almost empty. We stopped and looked around.

"Hi!" called a familiar voice from the back of the room.

It was the Rodowsky boys. And the Arnold twins. And Matt and Haley Braddock. They were beaming with excitement and holding up an elaborate sign that read "BSC".

"W-what?" gasped Kristy.

"Surprise!" everyone shouted.

"It's a surprise," cried Jackie Rodowsky, bouncing up (and letting one side of the sign go so that it almost flopped over on everybody). "Me and Archie thought it up. We wanted to thank you *specially* for being the greatest, most favourite babysitters in the world. We worked on it while Shea was doing his homework."

"I didn't find out until yesterday," said Shea. "Hey, Claudia! Here. Sit by me."

"Oh, wow! Great! But, um . . . could you give us a second?" I grabbed the two nearest arms, hissed "Come *on*!" and led the BSC into the ladies'. It was a tight fit, and it got even tighter when I ordered, "Get rid of the joke stuff and beautify yourselves. Now!"

Kristy usually gives the orders, but this time she obeyed without a word. So did everyone else, even Stacey.

"I don't believe this," muttered Jessi, pulling off the stained white T-shirt she'd been wearing and stuffing it in her bag along with a rubber chicken. She was wearing a plain leotard underneath.

"Watch your elbows," Mallory warned, trying to smooth her hair down.

I bent over and rolled the legs of my jeans shorts to equal lengths, then tucked the

132

shirt-tail into the waistband so the bleach mark didn't show. I rubbed off the orange lipstick and was trying to comb my hair when Kristy handed me a rubber band she'd taken out of her own hair (she'd been wearing a weird top-knot).

"Thanks," I said.

My eyes met Stacey's briefly in the mirror, but I couldn't tell what her expression was. I think that was partly because I looked away so quickly, and partly because Stacey was wearing so many different colours of eyeshadow.

Looking a little more presentable, we left the cloakroom.

"Hooray!" shouted Jackie, and I could feel myself blushing. We joined them sheepishly and sat down.

"I officially declare that this party will come to order," said Shea, scooting sideways to make a place for me.

Marilyn and Carolyn Arnold picked up the menus and began to hand them around proudly.

"This is on us," said Haley, translating in sign language for her brother Matt. (Matt can do some lip reading, but not when the person is facing away from him!)

"Anything you want!" signed Matt, grinning.

We all studied the menus and then

ordered a round of ice-cream sundaes, double fudge shakes, various cones with assorted sprinkles, ice-cream sodas, a diet soda (for Stacey) and frozen yoghurt with fresh fruit (for Dawn). We tried not to order too much, since it was the kids' treat, but they kept adding things to the order.

Jackie Rodowsky got extra fudge syrup on his sundae and on the front of his shirt.

None of the kids seemed to notice how oddly we'd been dressed. (And still were, sort of.) I hoped Mr Braddock, who I had spotted sitting in a booth in the far corner, keeping an eye on everything and smiling as he read the newspaper, hadn't noticed either.

"This is great," Shea kept saying.

"It really is," replied Mary Anne. "What a terrific surprise!"

"We fooled you," Matt signed.

"You certainly did," Kristy signed back, and Matt grinned.

"You didn't even guess the notes were from us, did you?" asked Haley.

"Not for a minute," said Jessi.

"Ha!" cried Jackie triumphantly. "And we kept the secret, too."

"Does this have anything to do with the way you were always hanging around when we babysat?" I asked.

"Yes," replied Jackie, blushing.

Carolyn looked at Marilyn then and nodded.

Carolyn began, "We've got . . ."

". . . a present for you," concluded Marilyn.

Jackie and Archie pulled out a big folder, opened it, and solemnly handed each of us a piece of paper with our own individual portrait on it.

"Archie and me coloured a lot of these. We wanted to get everything right. That's why we kept spying on you when you were with Shea."

"Thank you," I said. "Thank you very much."

"These are terrific," said Mary Anne, with a catch in her voice.

"You made me look just like Rapunzel," said Dawn, smiling, and holding up a portrait that showed a girl with very, very, very long blonde hair.

Carolyn looked pleased. "I helped with that one," she said.

Just then I felt a poke in my side. I looked at Shea, who glanced down sideways at the space between us in the booth. A folded piece of plain white paper lay there, with my name printed on the outside.

I picked it up, and holding it below the table, unfolded it carefully.

Dear Claudia,
Thank you for helping me. You really are the best.
Your friend friend,
Shea

I looked up. Shea was blushing. I was, too, a little. I was also a little choked up. The note had made me feel *so* good.

I caught Shea's eye, just for a moment and smiled at him.

Shea smiled back, and then poked me with his elbow and returned to his ice-cream.

We finished our treats, admiring the portraits as we did, and then Jackie, Archie, Shea, Carolyn, Marilyn, Haley and Matt began to work out how they were going to pay the bill.

"Do you need any help?" asked Stacey. "I'm pretty good with numbers."

"No," said Jackie firmly.

Haley began to count out the money. "How much do we tip?" she whispered to the others.

They bent over and Matt produced a pencil and began to write some numbers on the back of the bill. But then Shea, looking over his shoulder, suddenly said, "Three

136

dollars and twenty cents." He signed the answer to Matt, who looked surprised.

"Wow!" said Haley. "How did you do that?"

Shea shrugged. "I don't know."

I smiled to myself. "We'll meet you outside," I said.

Outside the restaurant, Mrs Braddock had just pulled up.

"Did you have a good time?" she called.

"It was a wonderful surprise!" I called back.

"For some wonderful babysitters," she answered.

We grinned. It is so nice to be appreciated!

Then the kids burst out of the restaurant.

"Does anyone need a lift?" asked Kristy, in her best chairman-of-the-BSC voice.

Mr Braddock laughed. "We're dropping the kids off. No babysitting work required, Kristy."

"This is absolutely, positively the nicest surprise I can imagine," said Mary Anne.

I looked up and met Stacey's eyes. What was she thinking? Would this soften her up or would she hate me for ever? "Absolutely," I said, and my fingers touched the note from Shea, which I'd put in my pocket.

"Yes," agreed Archie.

That broke the sentimental air that was settling over us all. We waved goodbye as the kids piled into the Braddocks' car.

"Thank you!" we called.

"See you soon," called Jackie, hanging out of the window. Our last sight of our secret admirers was of a hand yanking Jackie back in, before he could tumble out of the car.

14th CHAPTER

I was in a funny mood when I got home from our secret admirer surprise party. I was feeling really good about the party. But I was feeling really awful about Stacey and my secret journal.

I took Shea's note out of my pocket and looked at it again, smiling as I saw where he'd written *freind*, then crossed it out and written *friend*. "'I' before 'e' except after 'c'," I said aloud.

Then I opened my jewellery box and put the note in it with the other secret admirer notes—all the evidence. Evidence that we were good babysitters. Evidence that I was a good tutor, too. And evidence that I could be a friend.

And a friend was a friend no matter how you spelled it.

Closing the jewellery box, I flopped

down in the director's chair with the telephone. "This meeting of people who formerly had best friends will now come to order," I said.

I thought of digging out some kind of junk food to make it official, but I was suddenly too depressed. What was I going to do? Stacey hadn't said anything about the journal at the cafe but then, Stacey hadn't said anything to me at all. Officially, we still weren't speaking.

Maybe I could write her a note.

Or could I? What if I spelled something wrong?

On the other hand, I could just phone her.

The phone in my lap rang then and I jumped about fifty metres. I picked up the receiver. "Hello!" I yelped.

Stacey didn't even say hello. "We've got to talk."

"Oh! Yes. Ah . . ."

"Can you come over?"

"Okay," I said. "I'll be right there." Then I remembered what I was wearing and added, "In a few minutes."

"Good," said Stacey.

I changed into something more suitable—a giant blue-and-white striped shirt and socks with blue spots, with blue cycling shorts that matched the stripes and spots. I pulled on red Reeboks, and hung a dangly red earring made of a string of hearts in one ear and another earring that was a dangly row of silver arrows. I pulled my hair back with a red ribbon, and headed for Stacey's.

She'd changed, too, into black jeans and black Doc Marten's, and a big golden yellow shirt with round black buttons.

She looked super. But stern.

My heart sank.

Stop it, Claudia, I scolded myself. It's not your fault she read your journal.

But I was tired of worrying about whose fault it was. I wanted my best friend to be my best friend again. Not the Alien Wicked Tutor. And not angry with me.

"I'm sorry," I said.

"I'm sorry," Stacey said at the same time.

We both stopped, then started again.

"No, I . . ."

"But I . . ."

"Stace, listen . . ."

"Oh, Claud, did I really . . ."

And then we were both talking at once. It was funny. Each of us understood what the other was saying even though anyone listening to the—cacophony—probably wouldn't have been able to make any sense of it at all.

We stopped talking at the same time. We began to smile, a little.

"Okay," I said. "I'm sorry about what I wrote. I suppose you've realized by now that I was keeping two journals."

Stacey nodded. "Have I just!"

"Well, I was pretty angry. And I meant what I wrote, even though I knew you were just trying to help. I suppose, in a way, I hated to admit I needed help. Because for me, admitting I need help feels like I'm admitting I'm stupid. I suppose."

"Oh, Claud. You're not stupid! You're the most creative person I know. And clever."

"Not so clever about being a good best friend."

"Me, neither. What you wrote hurt, but it also had a lot of truth in it. I was treating you like some little kid. It was as if I expected you to act irresponsibly and misbehave. Then when you did complain, I did turn into the Weird Evil Alien Tutor." Stacey paused. "I'm sorry I was so tough on you that you had to keep a secret journal like that. But," she added slyly, "your spelling has improved!"

We both smiled. Then I said, "Your hard work paid off."

"It was your hard work, too," said Stacey.

"I know," I said. "I also know I'd like you to keep helping me. If you will."

"Okay," agreed Stacey.

We both paused. Then Stacey said, "Want to do some work now?"

I groaned.

Stacey didn't say anything.

"Yes," I said. "Reluctantly. And don't ask me to spell that!"

"I bet you could," replied Stacey, leading the way to her room.

By Tuesday, I couldn't study any more, even if the test hadn't been scheduled for that day. In fact, Stacey hadn't even let me study the night before. "Go over the words once," she ordered. "Then do something you enjoy."

So I did. I made a collage out of junk food wrappers. I'm going to put it with my series of junk food paintings and drawings.

As Mrs Hall handed out the tests the next day, I took deep breaths.

"You may begin," said Mrs Hall.

I pulled the sleeve of my shirt down over my watch. I wasn't going to think about the time. I wasn't going to panic.

Closing my eyes, I told myself, you know this stuff. You are not stupid.

And even if you don't know all the answers, you're still not stupid.

I opened my eyes and looked down at the first question—and I knew the answer.

143

I read the first question over twice, just to make sure I understood it. Then, slowly, carefully, without panicking, I began to do the test.

When I had finished, I still didn't look at my watch or the clock. The time wasn't important. Instead, I went back over my test, checking the questions and then the answers.

I was one of the last people to finish. But I had finished on time. As I handed my paper to Mrs Hall, I couldn't help but smile. I didn't want to be cocky, but I felt I had done really well.

Mrs Hall gave me a small, serious smile back.

It goes without saying that I was a pretty distracted student after that. I had trouble keeping my mind on my art lesson after school, and on the Wednesday BSC meeting. Thursday at school wasn't any better. I was actually counting the minutes until English class (and dreading it, too).

Thursday was when Mrs Hall had said she'd hand back the tests.

At last it was time. I clenched my hands in my lap as Mrs Hall passed the corrected tests back to us.

I took my test, unfolded it, and looked at the top of the paper.

B minus! I'd passed. And I would pass English, too.

I looked down the paper and gave a little gasp. On the spelling part of the test, I'd earned a 97! It was one of the highest grades I'd ever got in spelling.

I looked up and met Mrs Hall's eye. She nodded and smiled. Not a small, serious smile this time, but a big "congratulations" one.

Congratulations to me. And to Stacey and to Shea, too.

15th CHAPTER

With my grade in English nailed down (at least for the time being) and spring in the air (more or less), I felt like dancing. So when Austin Bentley asked me to the Spring Dance at the Community Centre, I said yes, yes, yes.

As it turned out, my friends and I all had dates to the dance—Dawn asked Pete Black, and Shannon Kilbourne was coming with a boy from her school.

I must say that when Austin and I arrived at the Community Centre, and I checked out the other members of the BSC, we looked a lot better than we had outside the Rosebud Cafe waiting for our secret admirers.

Everyone else in Stoneybrook seemed to have caught a little spring dance fever, too. The crowd was huge. And since the first part of the dance was supposed to be a spring party, that meant that families and kids were there, too, including lots of our clients.

"Oh, look!" I exclaimed.

Austin looked, and did a, well, double-take: Carolyn and Marilyn were dancing— with two of the Pike triplets. Vanessa Pike was standing nearby, staring at the twin girls dancing with two of the triplets. I could tell by Vanessa's expression that she was thinking of some poetic tribute to the sight.

"Want to dance?" I asked Austin, and we hurried on to the dance floor as Jackie Rodowsky and Hannie Papadakis hopped by in their socks.

"What are you doing?" I asked.

"The sock hop," said Hannie seriously.

My eyes met Austin's and I thought we would both burst out laughing, but we controlled ourselves until Jackie and Hannie had hopped out of hearing.

We danced over to the refreshment table. Bart and Kristy were there, and they began to talk to Austin about baseball and spring training.

"Have you seen Jenny Prezzioso?" asked Stacey, joining me while Sam scoured the refreshment table.

"No," I said, shaking my head.

"A vision in lavender," said Stacey. "It's

quite sweet, actually. She's even wearing a little corsage made of violets."

"It does sound sweet," I agreed. Jenny Prezzioso has more clothes than anyone—even any adult—I know. Her mother's very fussy about how Jenny dresses, and so is Jenny.

I smiled. How would Stacey and I dress our children, I wondered. Would we go for cute? Or something trendier? Maybe rompers in basic East Village New York baby black for Stacey. And something a little more colourful for me . . .

Across the room, I caught a glimpse of Mary Anne, sitting next to Mrs Newton. Mary Anne was holding Lucy, Jamie Newton's baby sister, in her arms. I was too far away to see what Lucy was wearing, apart from a blanket and a cap. But as we watched, Jamie approached his mother and executed a formal bow. Mrs Newton said something to Mary Anne, who nodded. Then Jamie and his mother stepped on to the dance floor.

"Cool," said Stacey.

Watching Mrs Newton and Jamie gave me an idea. "Would you lot excuse me for a moment?" I asked. I walked around the edge of the room until I spotted Shea Rodowsky.

"Shea!" I said.

He turned and grinned. "Hi!"

"Do you want to dance?" I asked.

Shea looked a little surprised. "Really? Okay!"

We began to foxtrot, sort of like Jamie and Mrs Newton were doing.

"This isn't bad," said Shea, after a minute.

"Thanks," I said.

"You're welcome." Shea wriggled his eyebrows and I wriggled mine at him like Groucho Marx. Then he said, "School isn't so bad now, either. I mean, you know, for school and all."

"I'm glad to hear it," I told him. "That's sort of the way I feel, too. And guess what? I passed my test."

"That's great!" said Shea.

"I did best on the spelling part," I said. "I wanted to thank you for helping me with my spelling. The things you told me helped a lot."

"Did they?" Shea looked really pleased. "We're not so stupid, then, huh?"

"No," I said. "The stupid ones are the people who think *we're* stupid."

"They'd better watch out," said Shea. He added, "My report card was better, too."

"Super. Extra super."

"Yeah. They told me I was 'challenged'. Now that I'm getting better at all the school stuff, I don't mind the teachers and the tutors helping me so much."

I thought for a minute, then said, "Well, I liked getting a good grade for my test, so if I ever need help again, I'm going to get it."

Shea looked up at me and his eyes gleamed. "Even in the resource room?"

"Well . . . let's just call it the challenged room," I answered.

Shea made a face at me and I made a face back and the music ended.

"Thank you," I said to Shea. "Thank you for being a special friend."

"Aw," said Shea. He ducked his head, slid off the dance floor, and was swallowed up by a group of his friends standing nearby.

A few minutes later, the crowd began to thin out and change as the younger kids were gathered together to be taken home. I had a chance to look around again, and admire the decorations in all the spring colours. I felt as if I were inside an Easter egg looking out.

The music changed and the lights became softer.

I saw Jessi and Curtis Shaller and waved. Kristy and Bart were still standing by the refreshments, only now Pete Black and Dawn were talking to them. Logan pulled Mary Anne to her feet and headed for the dance floor, while Mallory and Ben Hobart crashed down in a chair nearby, laughing. Stacey drifted by with Sam, her head on his shoulder. She gave me a dreamy smile and I knew we'd be on the phone talking about Sam and the dance and the evening before the night was over. I was glad to have my best friend back.

All was right with the world, and I wasn't about to argue with it.

"Feel like dancing?" asked Austin, reaching for my hand.

"Do I?" I answered. "Definitely!"

Are you following the Babysitters Club Mysteries series?

Look out for:

BABYSITTERS LITTLE SISTER

Meet Karen Brewer. She's seven years old and her big sister Kristy runs the Babysitters Club. And Karen's always having adventures of her own . . . Read all about her in her very own series.

The Outfit — Robert Swindells

"Faithful, fearless, full of fun,
Winter, summer, rain or sun,
One for five, and five for one –
THE OUTFIT!"

Meet The Outfit—Jillo, Titch, Mickey and Shaz. Share in their adventures as they fearlessly investigate any mystery, and injustice, that comes their way . . .

Move over, Famous Five, The Outfit are here!

The Secret of Weeping Wood

The Outfit are determined to discover the truth about the eerie crying, coming from scary Weeping Wood. Is the wood really haunted?

We Didn't Mean To, Honest!

The marriage of creepy Kenneth Kilchaffinch to snooty Prunella could mean that Froglet Pond, and all its wildlife, will be destroyed. So it's up to The Outfit to make sure the marriage is off . . . But how?

Kidnap at Denton Farm

Farmer Denton's new wind turbine causes a protest meeting in Lenton, and The Outfit find themselves in the thick of it. But a *kidnap* is something they didn't bargain for . . .

The Ghosts of Givenham Keep

What is going on at spooky Givenham Keep? It can't be haunted, can it? The Outfit are just about to find out . . .